# KERMIT
# THE
# HERMIT

*written and illustrated by*

# BILL PEET

HOUGHTON MIFFLIN COMPANY BOSTON

To
my wife MARGARET
and my sons
BILL and STEVE

COPYRIGHT © 1965 BY WILLIAM PEET
COPYRIGHT © RENEWED 1993 BY WILLIAM B. PEET
All rights reserved. For information about permission
to reproduce selections from this book, write to
Permissions, Houghton Mifflin Company, 215 Park Avenue
South, New York, New York 10003.
LIBRARY OF CONGRESS CATALOG CARD NO. 65-20482.
ISBN: 0-395-15084-1 REINFORCED EDITION
ISBN: 0-395-29607-2 PAPERBOUND EDITION
PRINTED IN THE UNITED STATES OF AMERICA
WOZ  20

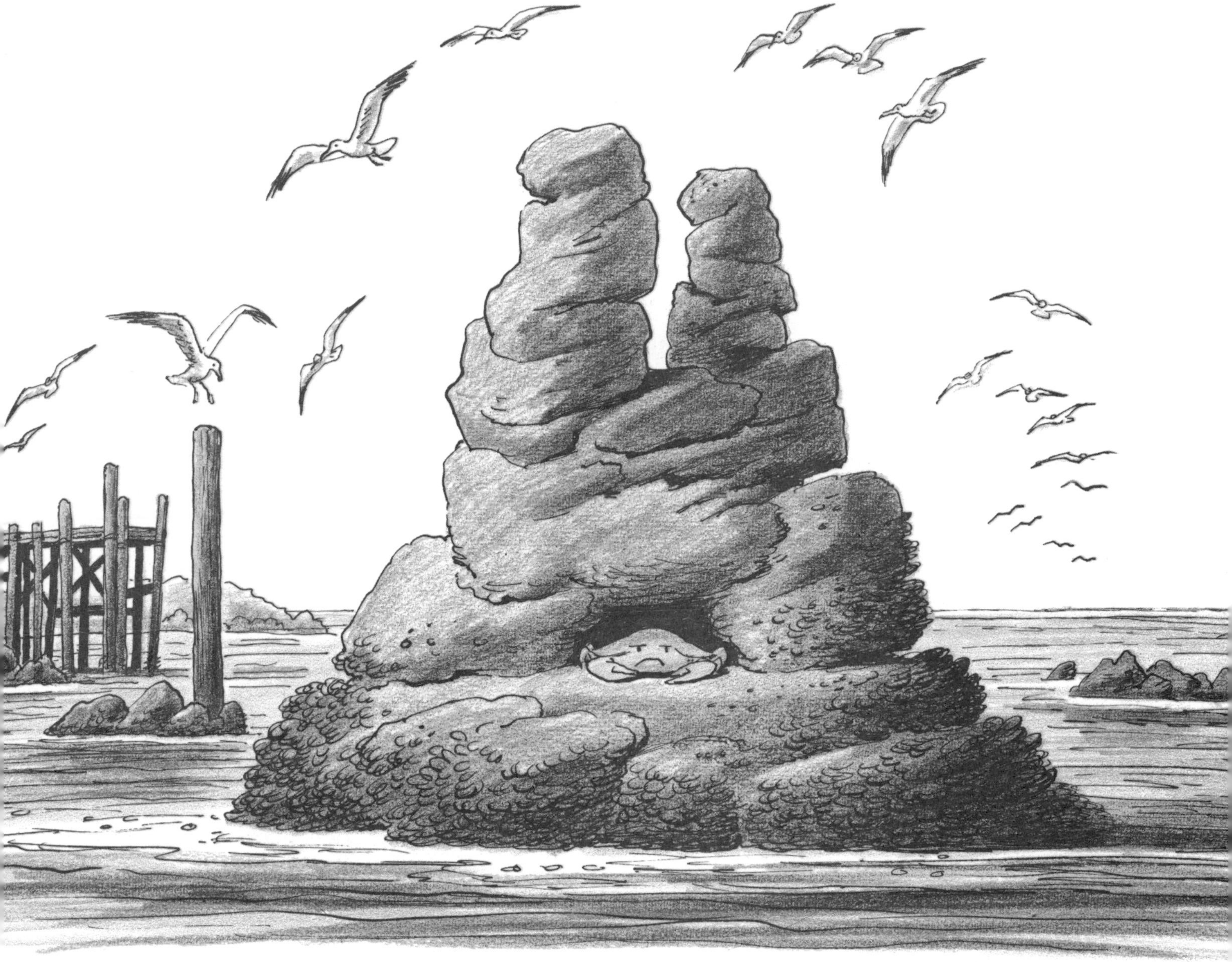

In Monterey Bay there's a jumble of rock
Stacked up like a castle across from the dock.
The king of this castle, an old crab called Kermit,
Lived all by himself in a cave like a hermit.
There was never a crab who was one half as selfish
Or one tenth as mean as this crusty old shellfish.

What made Kermit greedy and grumpy that way
Was the shortage of food everywhere in the bay,
For a crab must depend on what he can find—
Small scraps and tidbits of any old kind.
To Kermit each day meant a fight for survival
With every last seagull and crab as a rival.

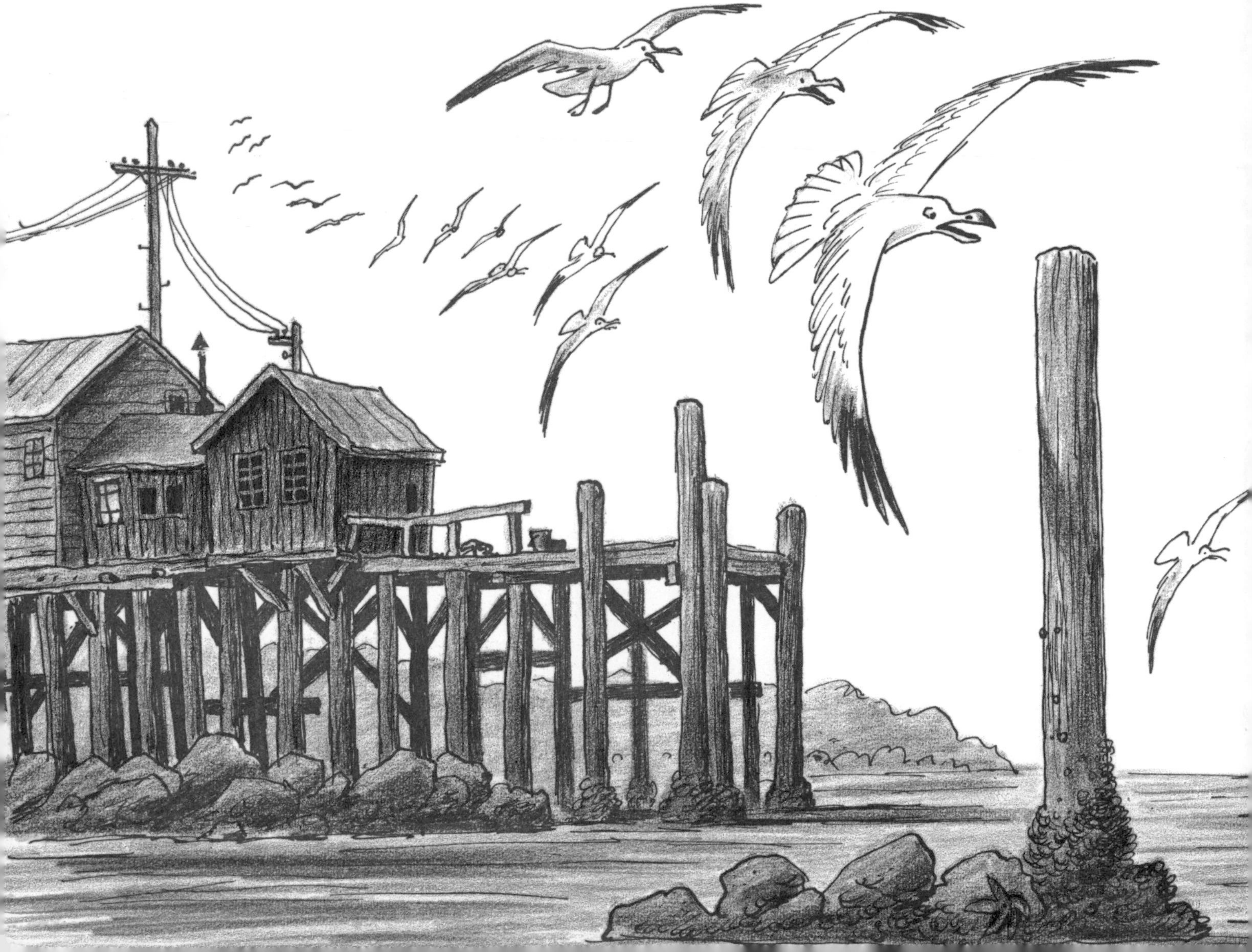

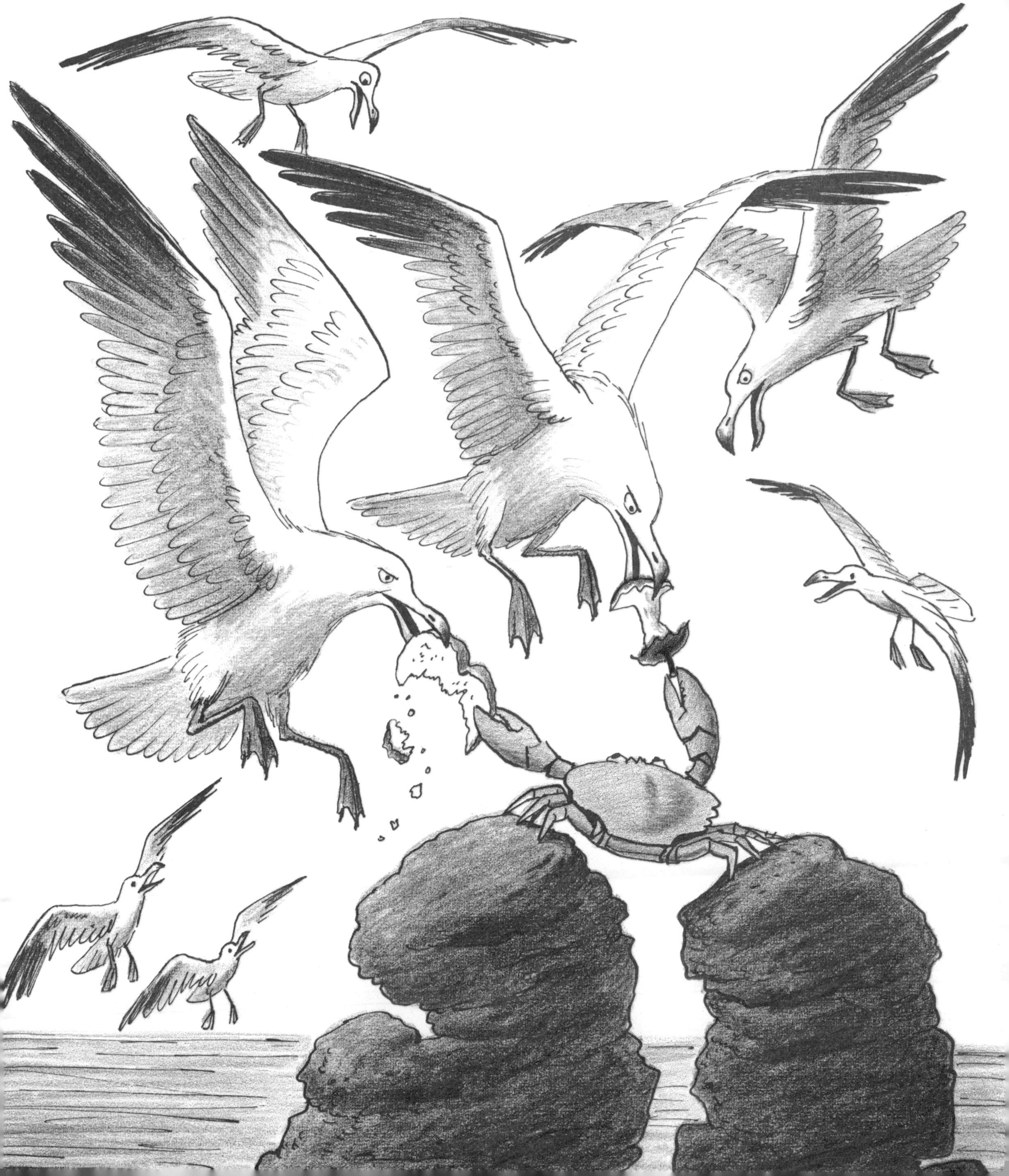

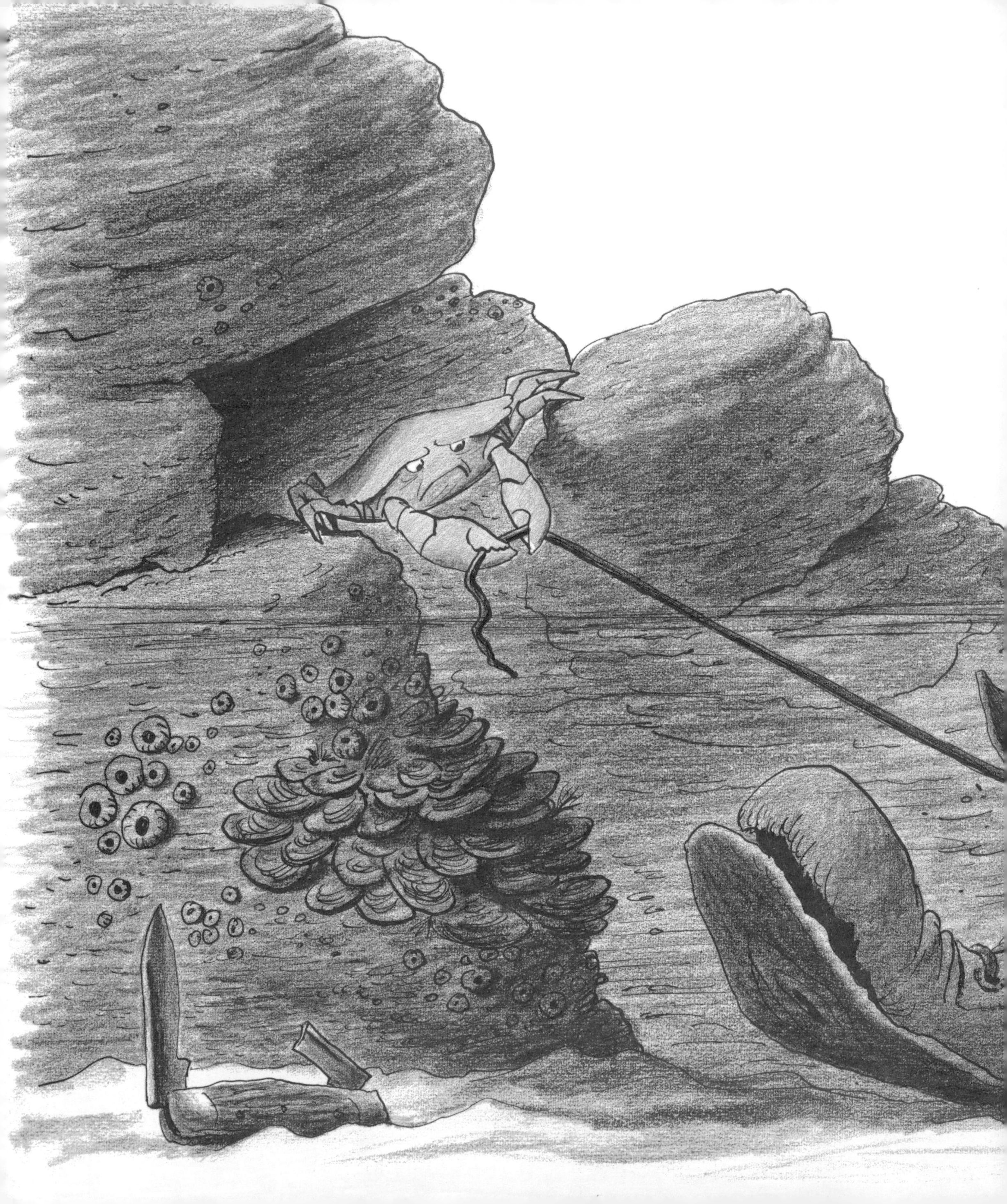

Unless it is cured sometimes greediness grows
Where it finally stops, alas, nobody knows;
And before very long Kermit grabbed everything
From a rusty padlock to a ball of kite string,
A broken jackknife, a pair of old shoes,
Things that a crab couldn't possibly use.

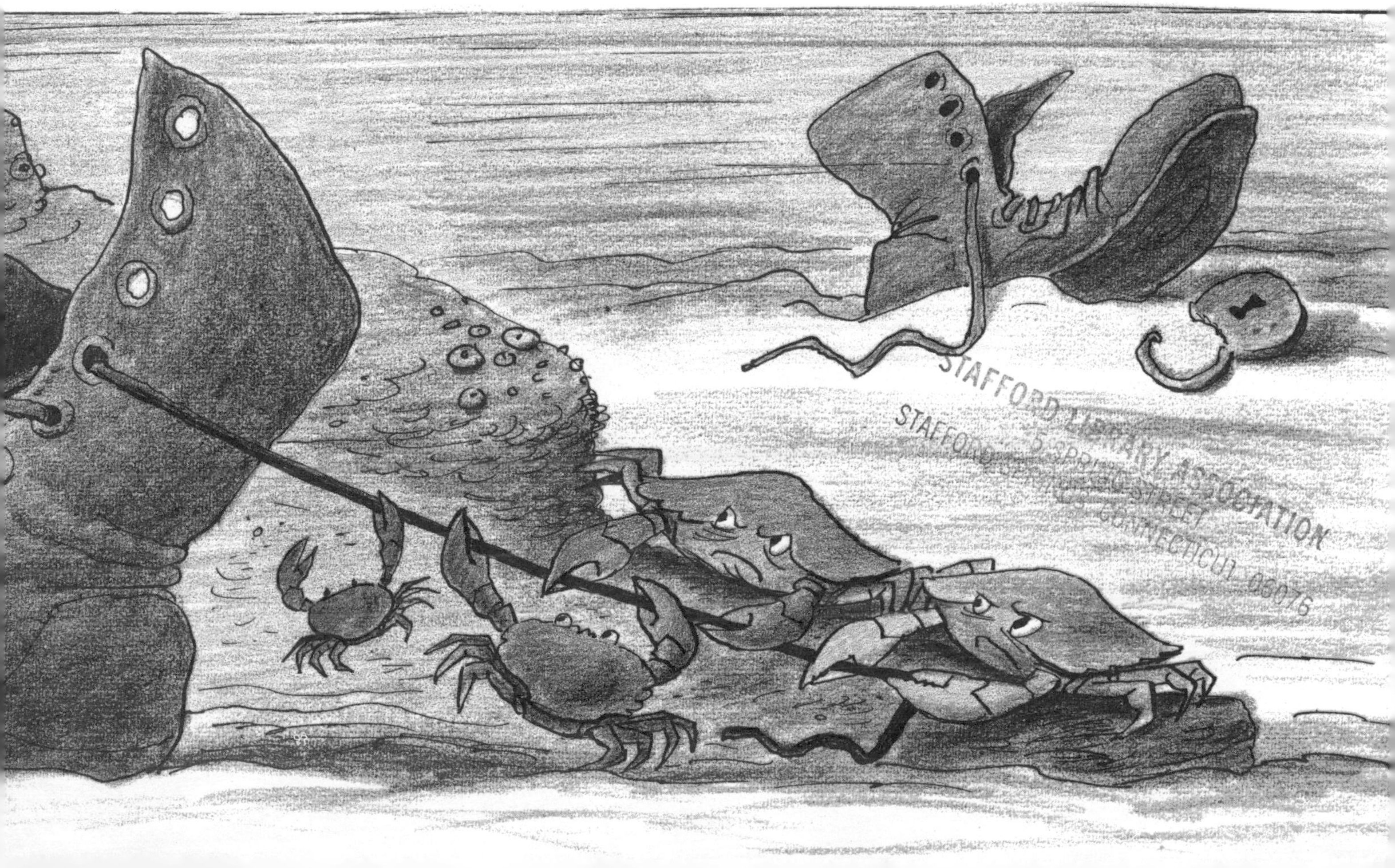

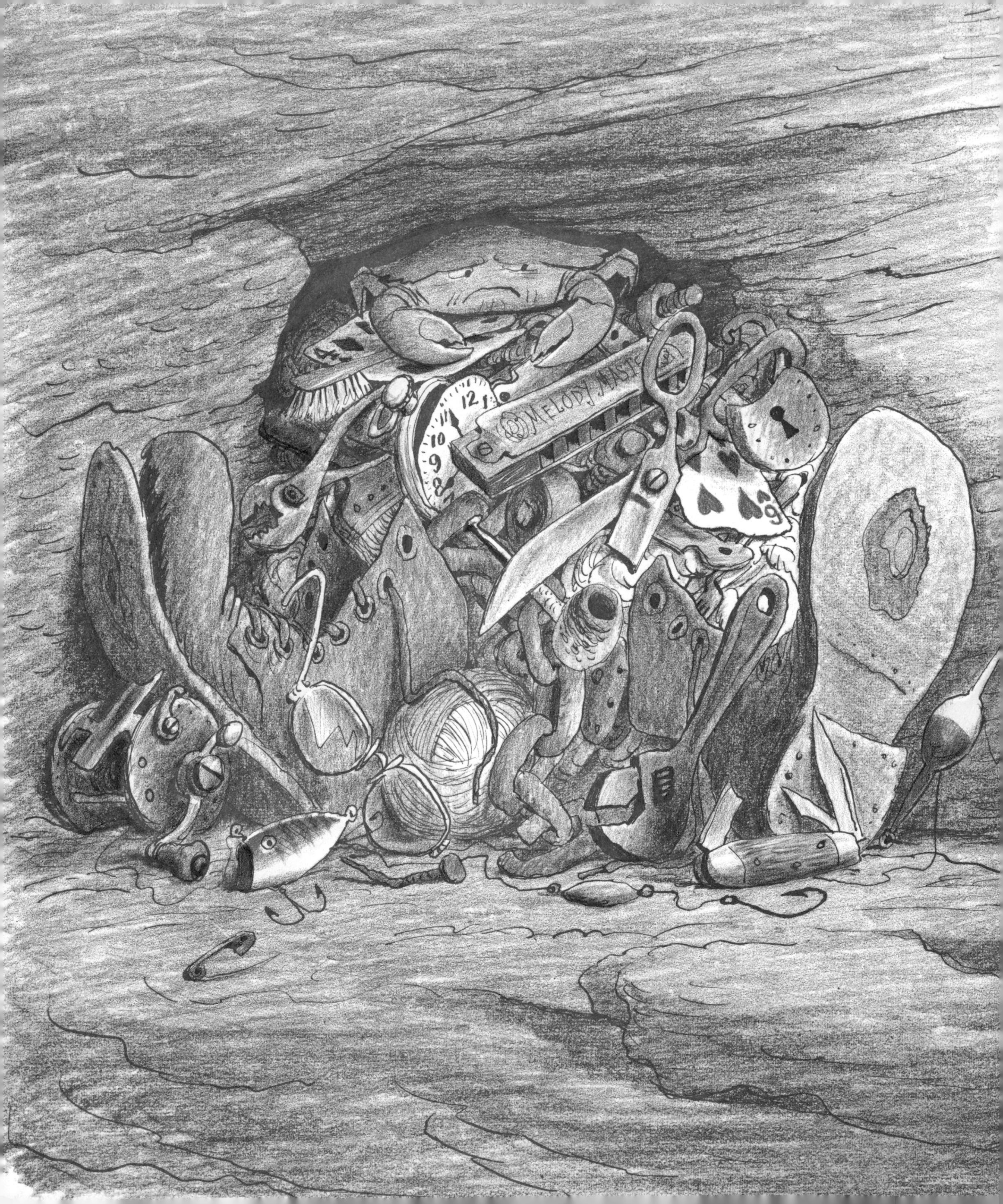
MELODY MASTE

And his cave was soon crammed without one inch to spare
There was just enough space left for Kermit in there.
Like any old miser he wanted a lot
Of something or other, he didn't care what;
And he'd have been greedy the rest of his days
If an odd twist of fate hadn't changed Kermit's ways.

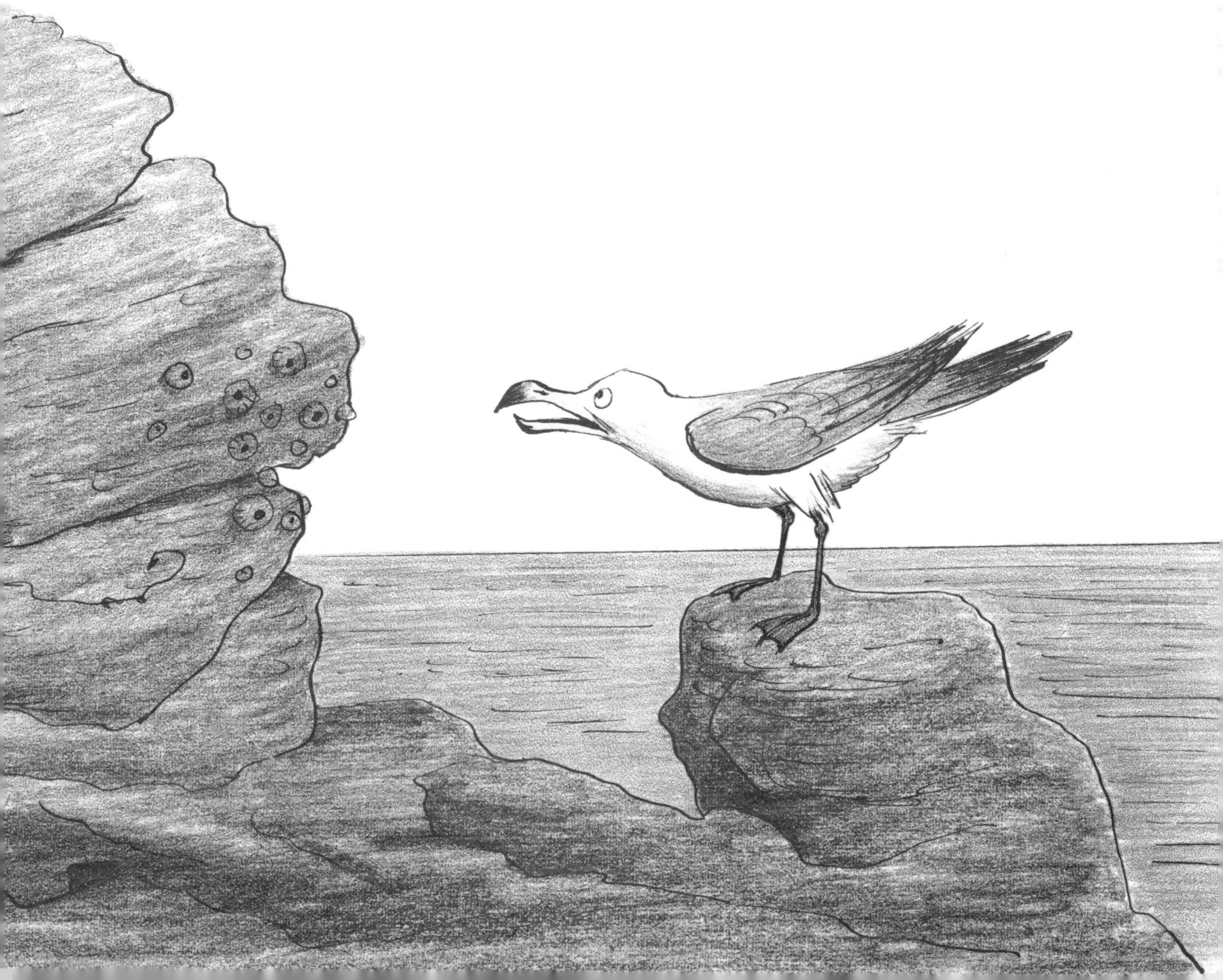

This remarkable change in old Kermit began
With an everyday thing, just a battered tin can,
A pork and bean can that had been tossed away
Far out in the sand dunes that bordered the bay.
The crumpled tin lid caught the sun's bright reflection
Which caused it to sparkle in every direction,
And since the old miser had never been told
That bright things that glitter are not always gold
He supposed that it must be some valuable thing
That someone had lost, a gold watch or a ring;
So he crawled off the rocks and out onto the land
Then over the hilly broad stretches of sand,

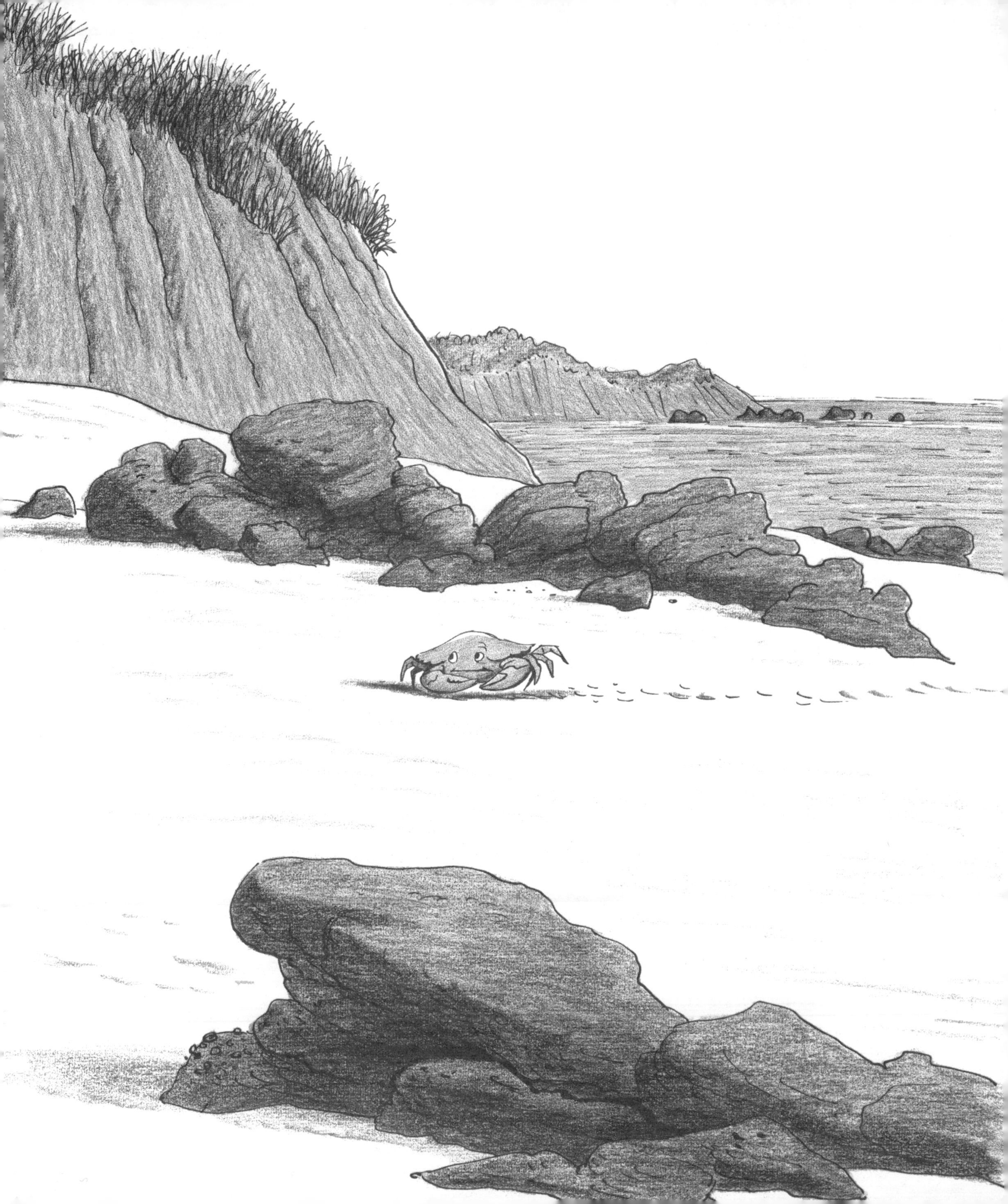

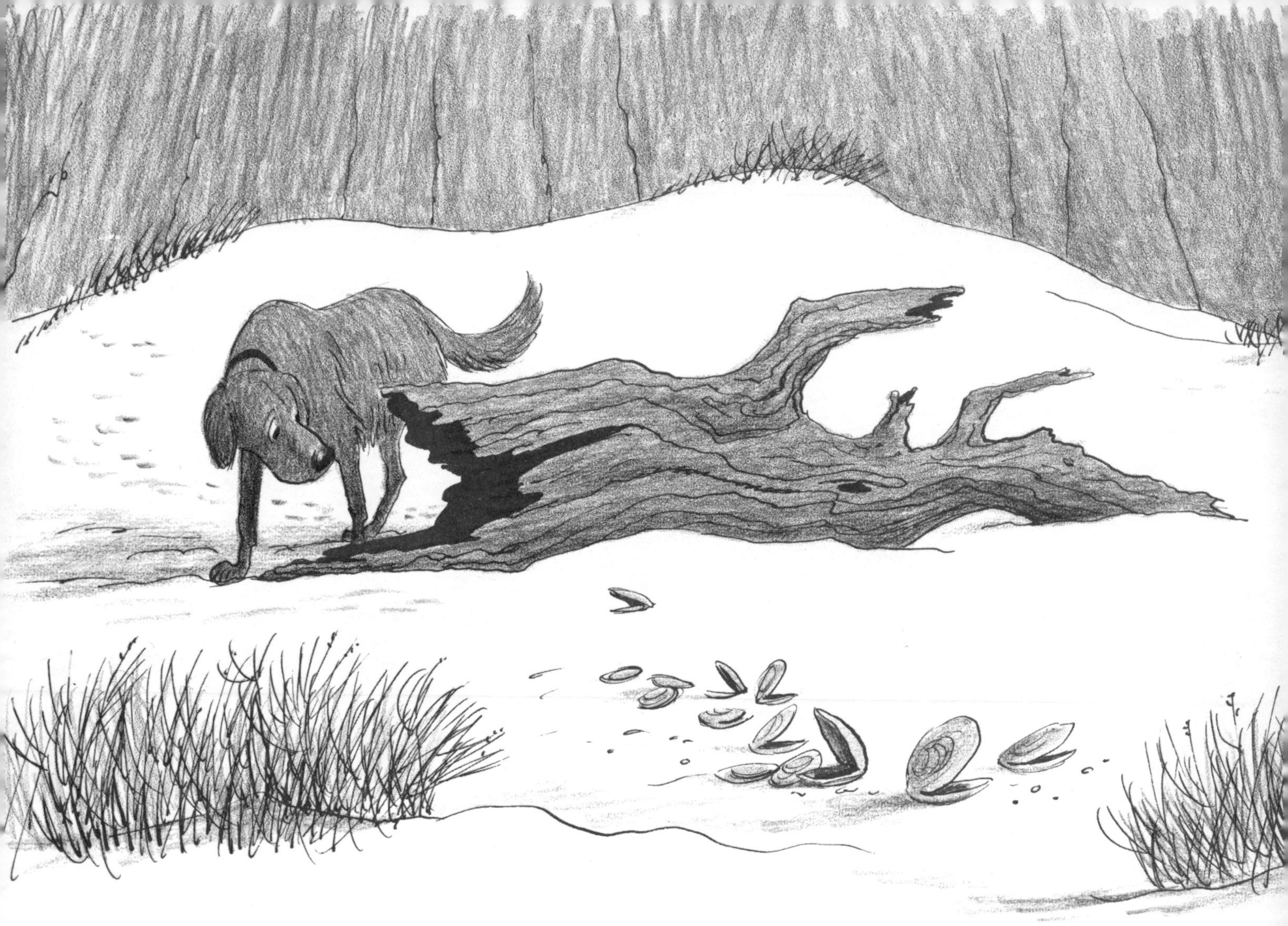

And not until Kermit was next to his prize
Did he realize a trick had been played on his eyes.
"Why you phoney tin faker, you," growled the old grump,
"Rubble like you should be tossed in a dump."
Then just as he turned to start back for the bay
The crab spied a dog who was heading his way.
The dog was exploring and trying out smells
Sniffing at driftwood and empty clam shells.

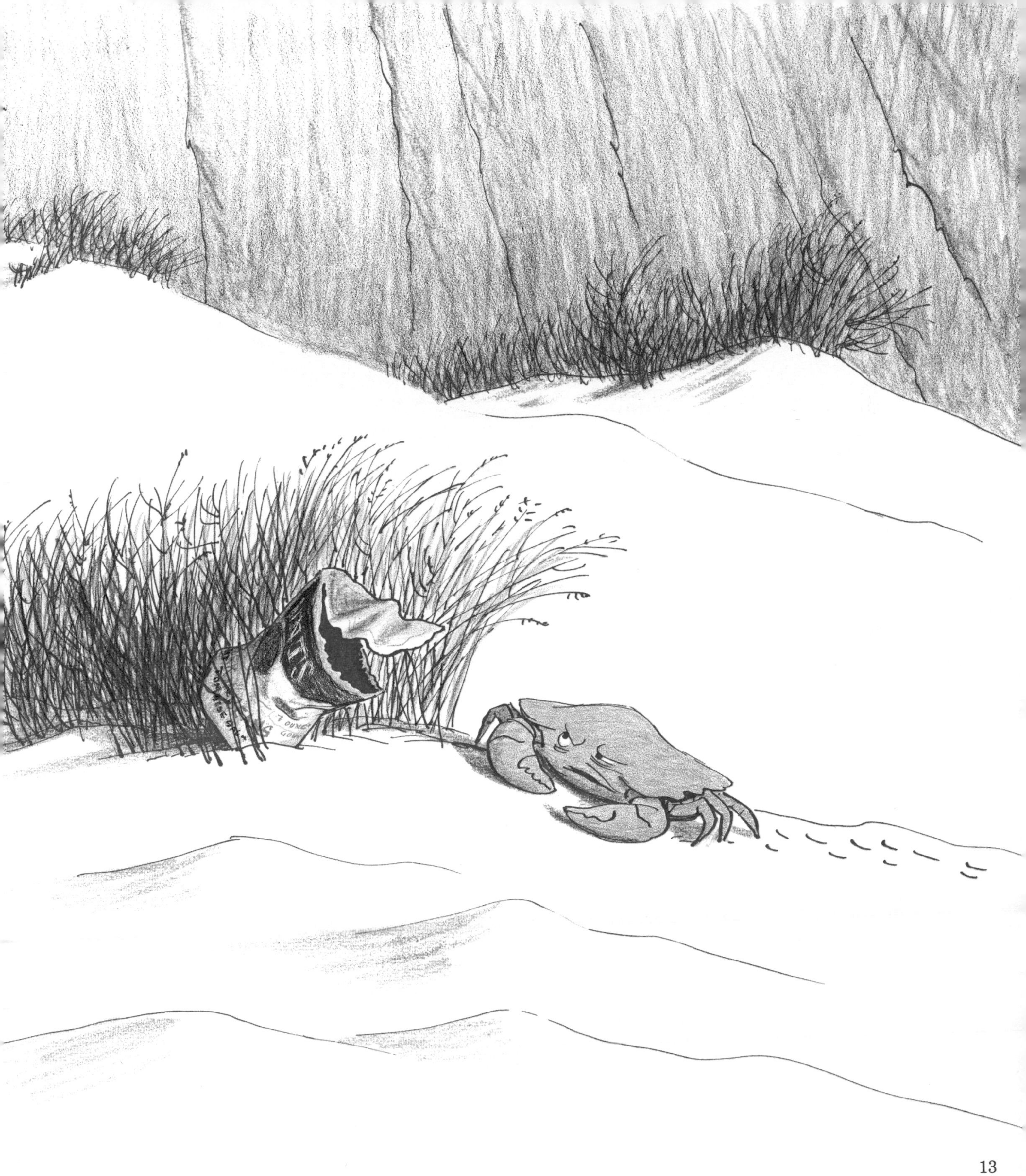

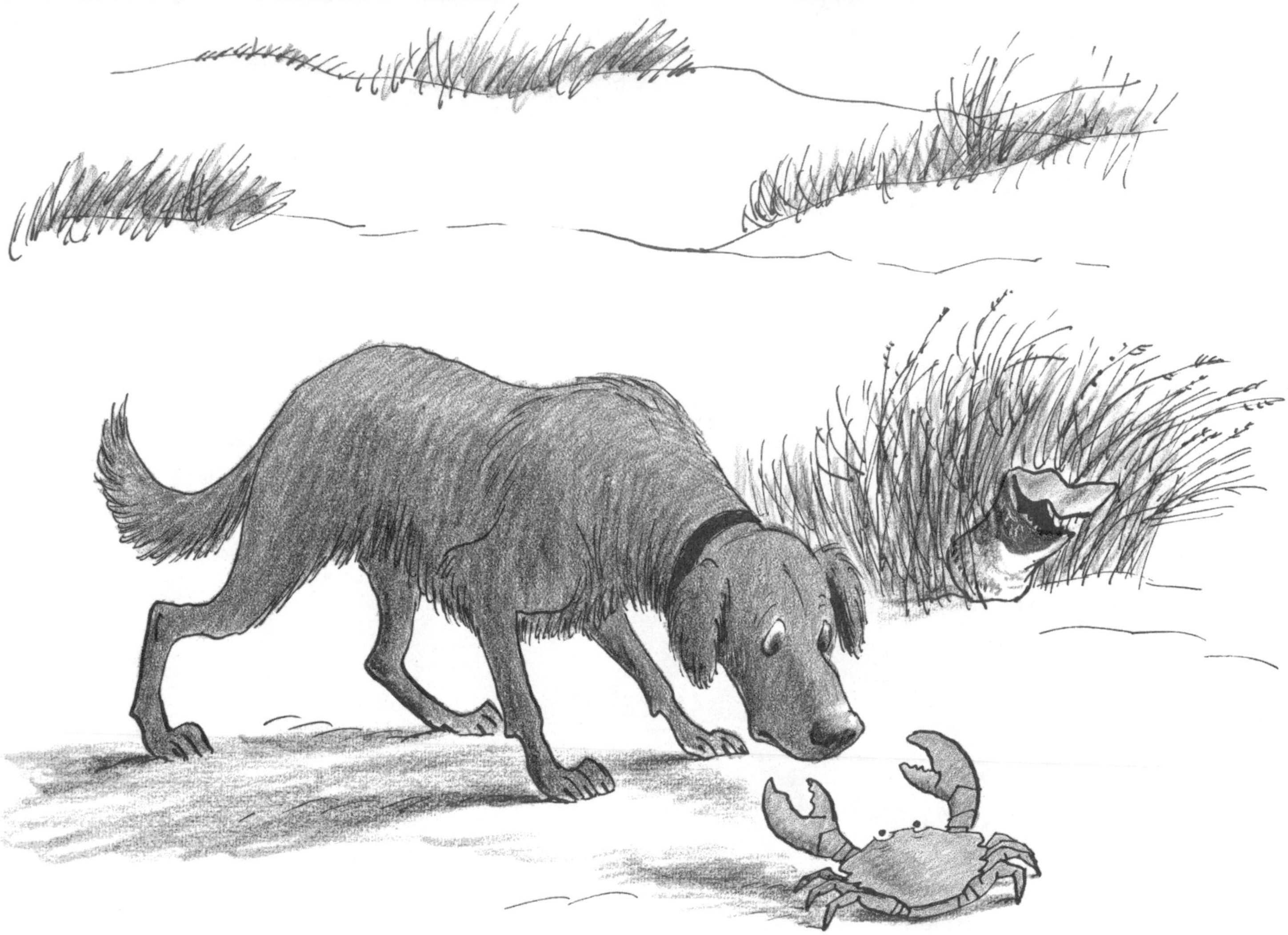

One sniff at the can told him what had been in it
So he then turned to sniff at old Kermit a minute.
In one grab the crab gave the dog a sharp nip
On his sensitive nose and he let out a "yip!"
"That'll teach you," he snapped, "to go sniffing at me."
Then he turned himself round to head back for the sea;
But the dog made a leap, seized the crab in his jaws
By the back of the shell, beyond reach of the claws.

"Put me down!" cried the crab, "Put me down, you big brute!
"Or I'll give you another good pinch on the snoot!"
But the dog paid no heed to old Kermit's command
He set to work digging a hole in the sand.
The crab guessed at once it was not just a cave
It was going straight down, so it must be a grave.
"What a horrible end," Kermit said with a groan,
"To be buried alive like a worthless old bone."

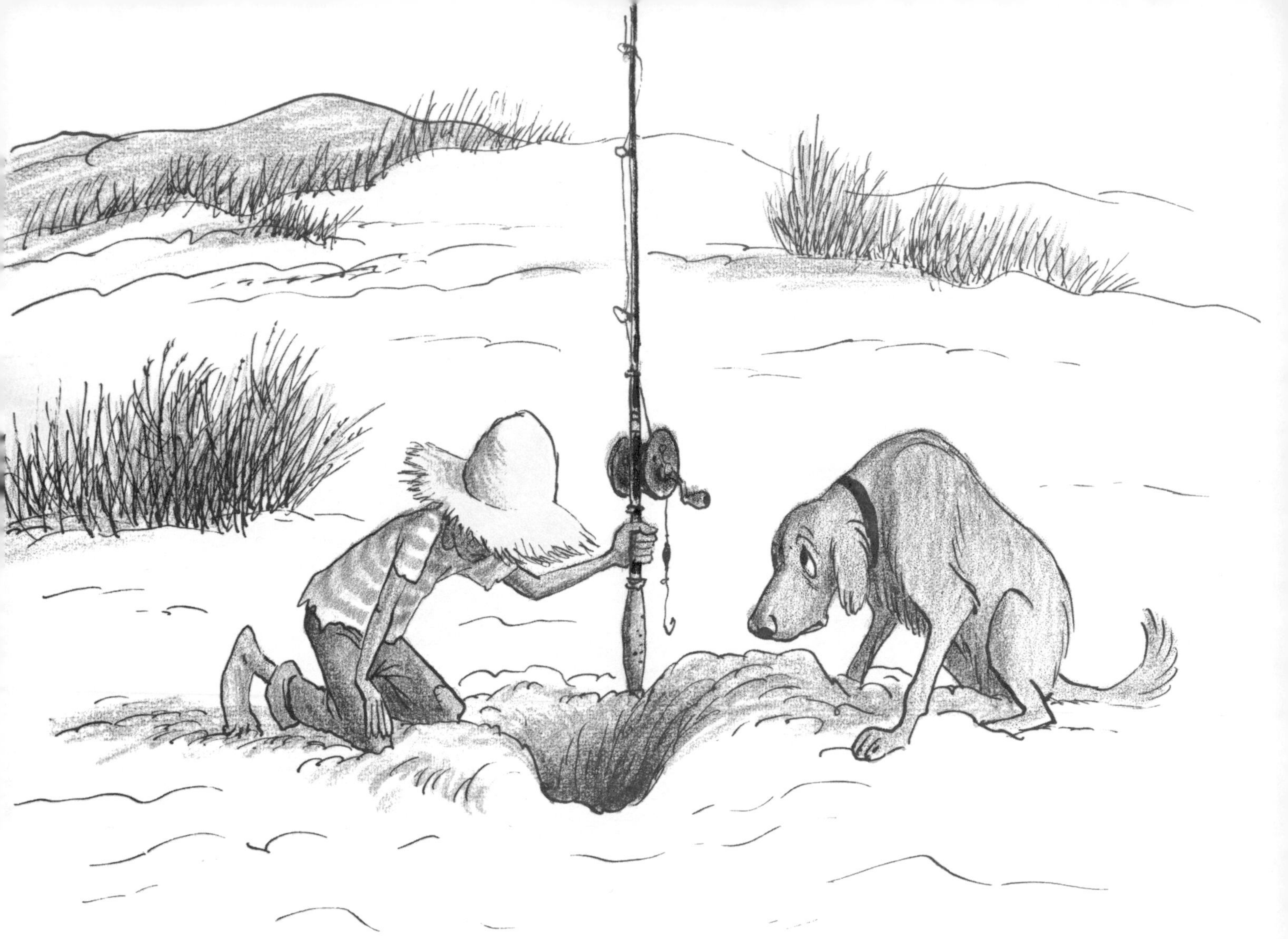

Then just as the dog dropped the crab in the hole,
A boy happened by with a long fishing pole.
"You old hound," he scolded, "what a mean thing to do.
"Now how would you like it if I buried you?

"You're too nice a dog to do something like that."
Then he scooped up the crab in his tattered straw hat,
Trotted off down the beach to the edge of the sea,
And flipping his hat he set old Kermit free.

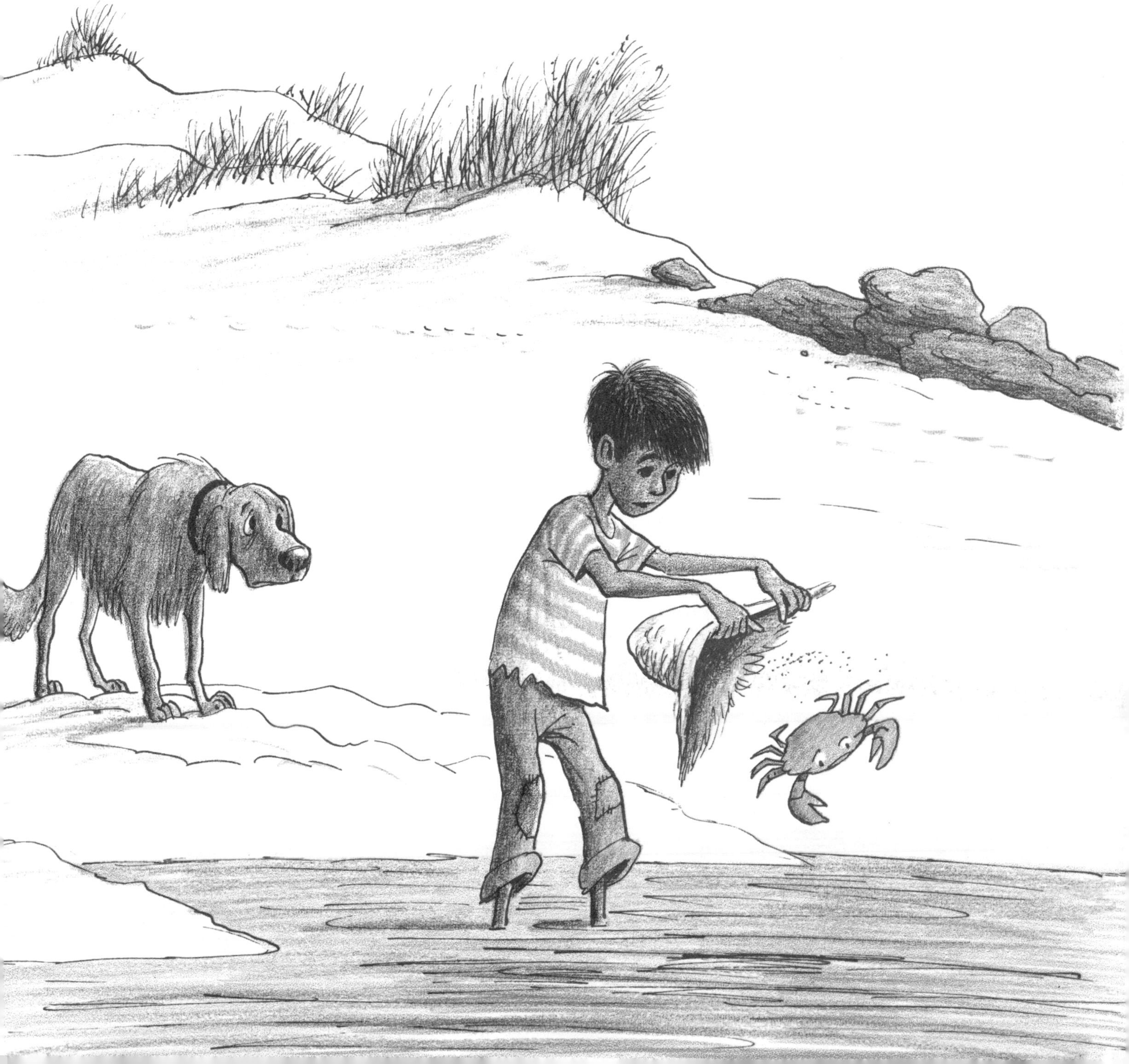

With a sigh of relief the old crab went his way
On back to his castle of rocks in the bay.
If it weren't for the boy he just had to admit,
There'd be no tomorrow, that would have been it.
"I'll reward my young friend," said old Kermit, "that's what
"With all my life savings, every last thing I've got.
"But things like old shoes or a broken jackknife
"Could never repay him for saving my life.
"The ideal reward would be a new bike
"There's something I'm sure that a small boy would like.
"Yet how can a crab ever buy a bicycle
Without any money, not even a nickel?"
He pondered the problem the whole afternoon
Then far into the night by the light of the moon;
But try as he might, alas and alack,
He thought of no way he could pay the boy back.

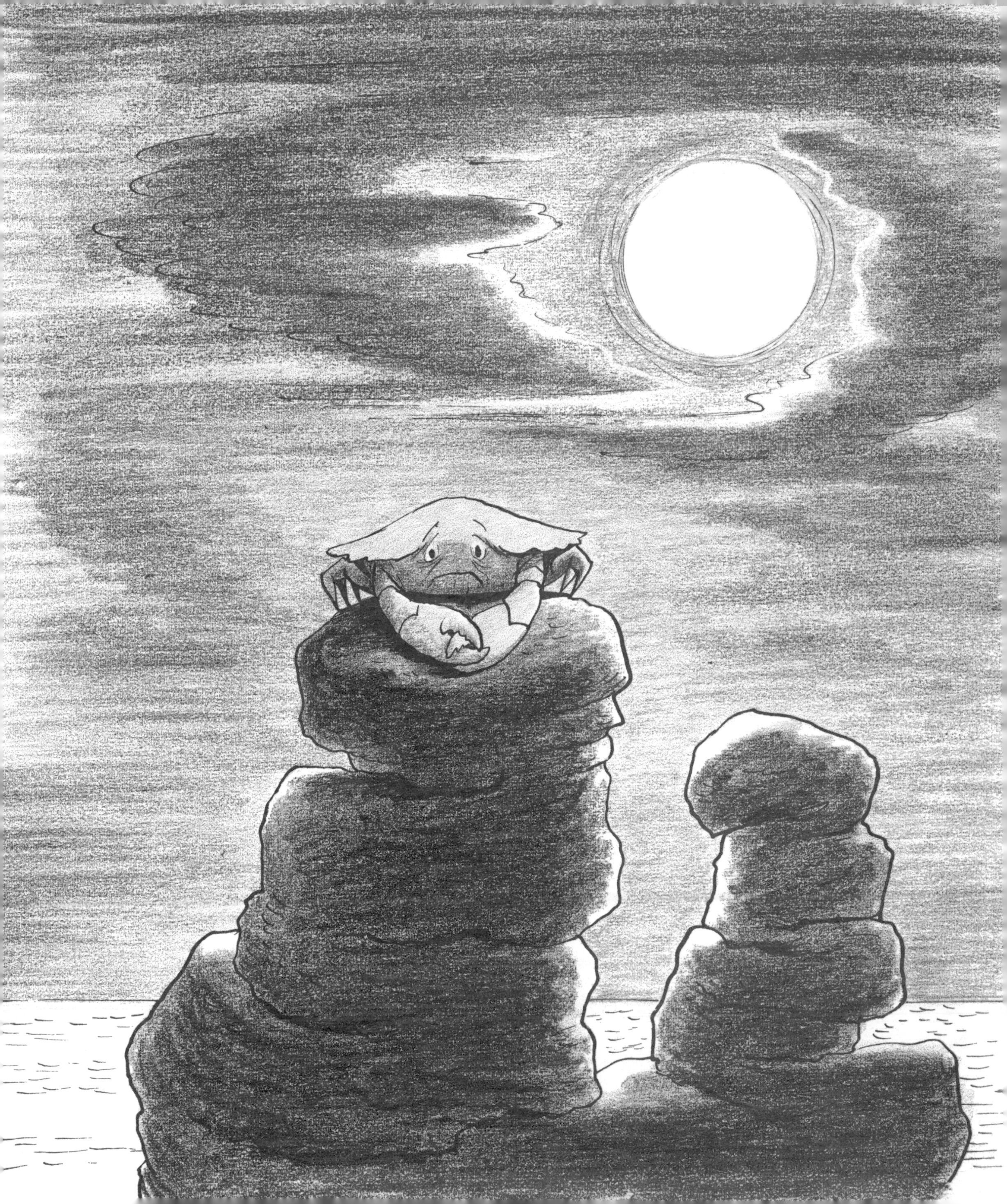

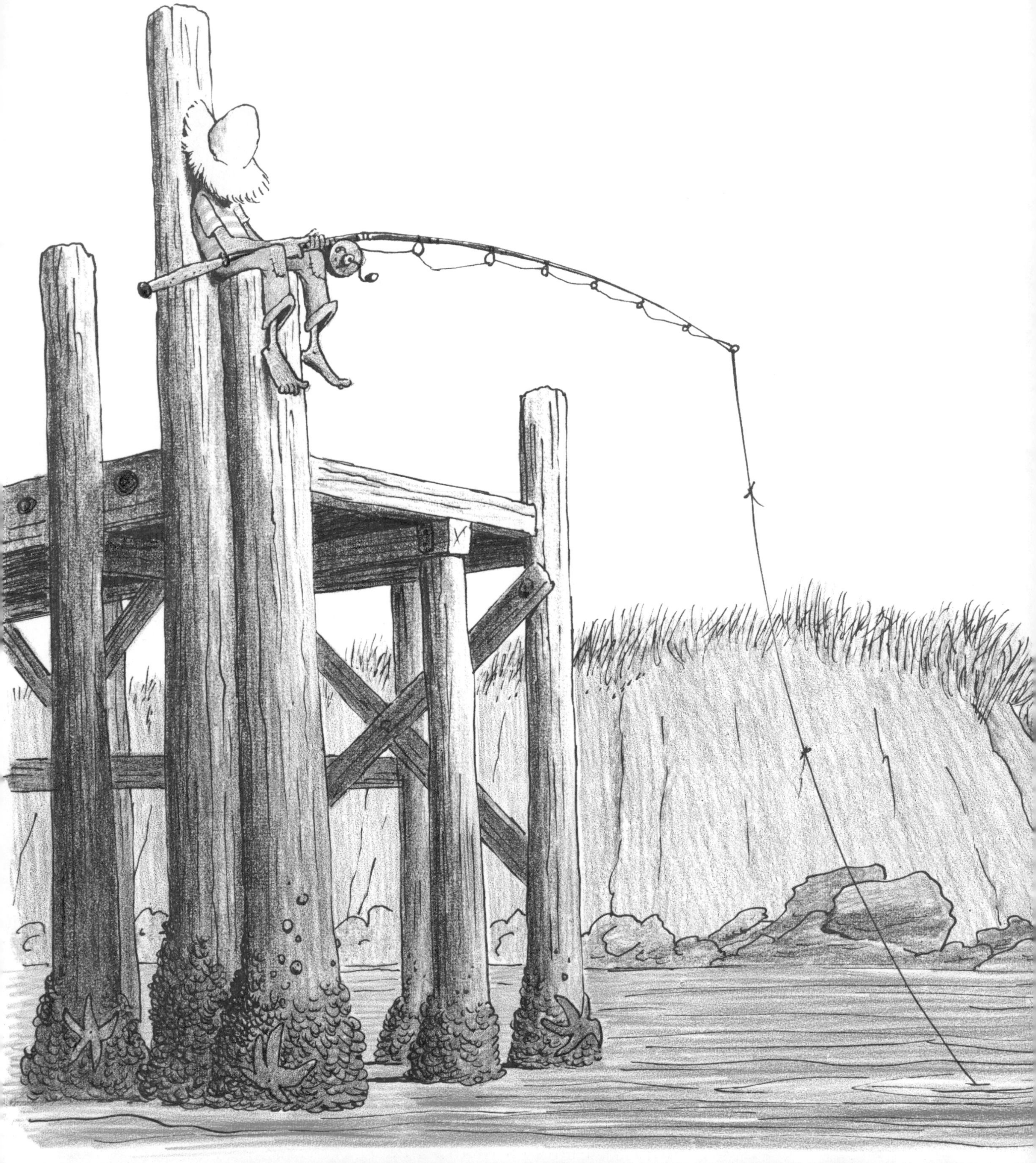

The next afternoon as he crawled on the rocks
Kermit spotted the boy on the end of the docks,
The very same boy, the old crab could tell that
By the faded striped shirt and the tattered straw hat.
He had been lulled to sleep by the warm summer breeze
With his fishing pole propped on his patched trouser knees.
"I might help him to catch a big fish," Kermit thought,
"If there's any big fish around here to be caught."

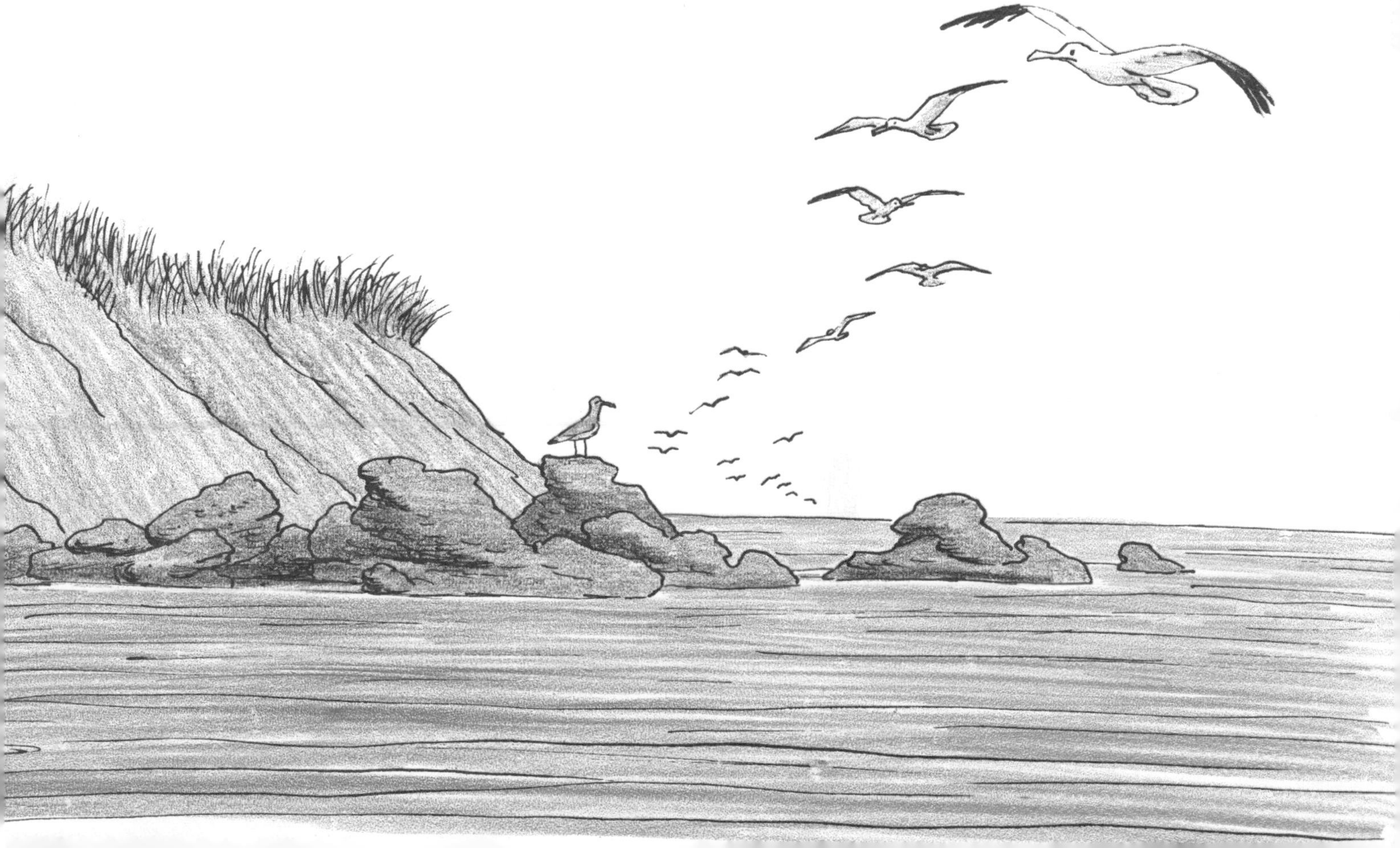

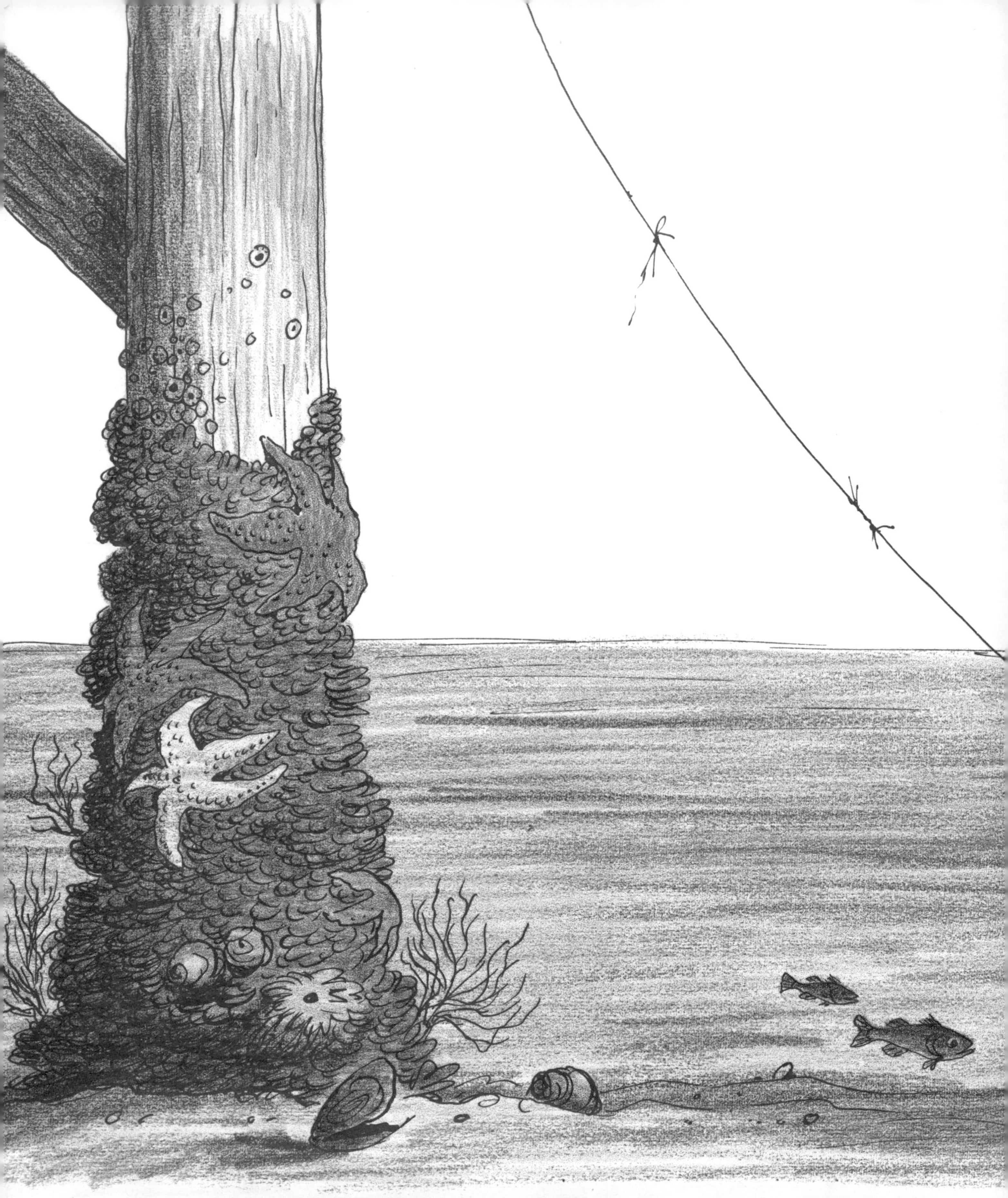

Of course he must first find the boy's baited hook,
So he scrambled out into the bay for a look,
And just a few yards from the pilings he found it
With a school of small minnows all swarming around it.
Lightly gripping the line just below the lead weight
Kermit tiptoed along gently dragging the bait.
If he happened to give it the least little jerk,
The boy would reel in and his plan wouldn't work.

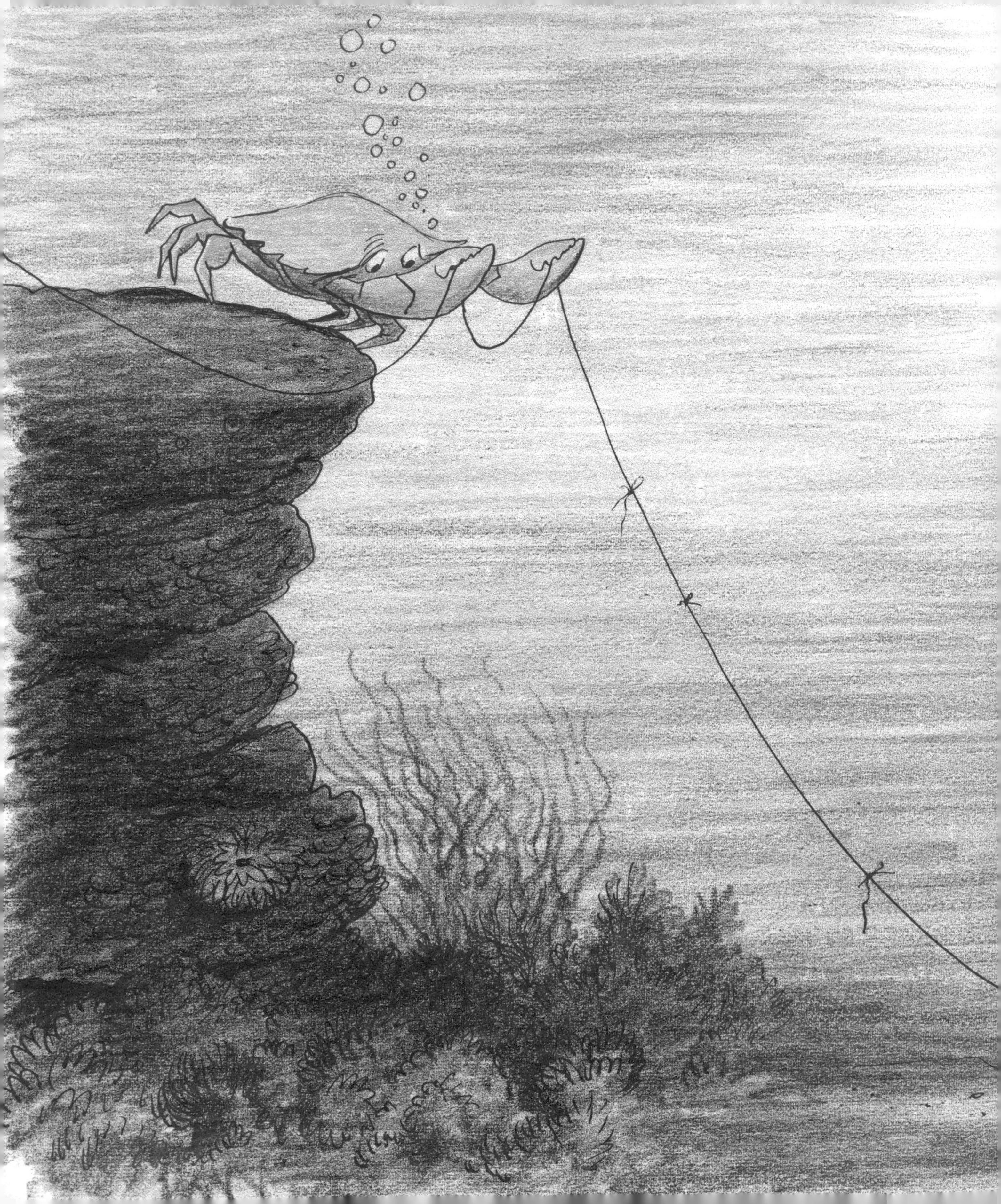

So Kermit kept on till he came to a ledge
Where he stopped to peer cautiously over the edge.
Then reaching as far as he could with his claws
He lowered the bait toward a halibut's jaws.
The big fish took a look and in one mighty scoop
Both the worm and the hook disappeared in one "gloop!"

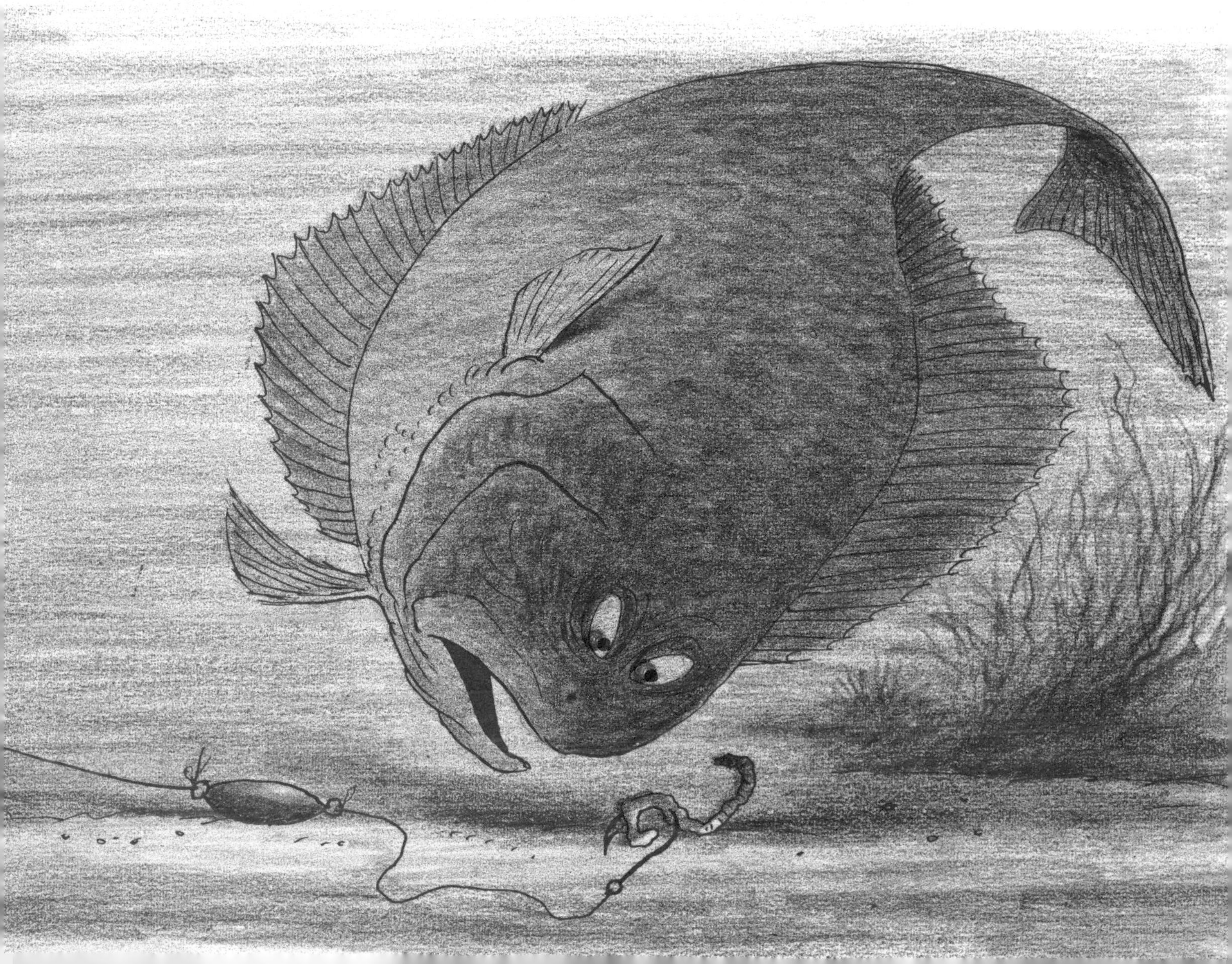

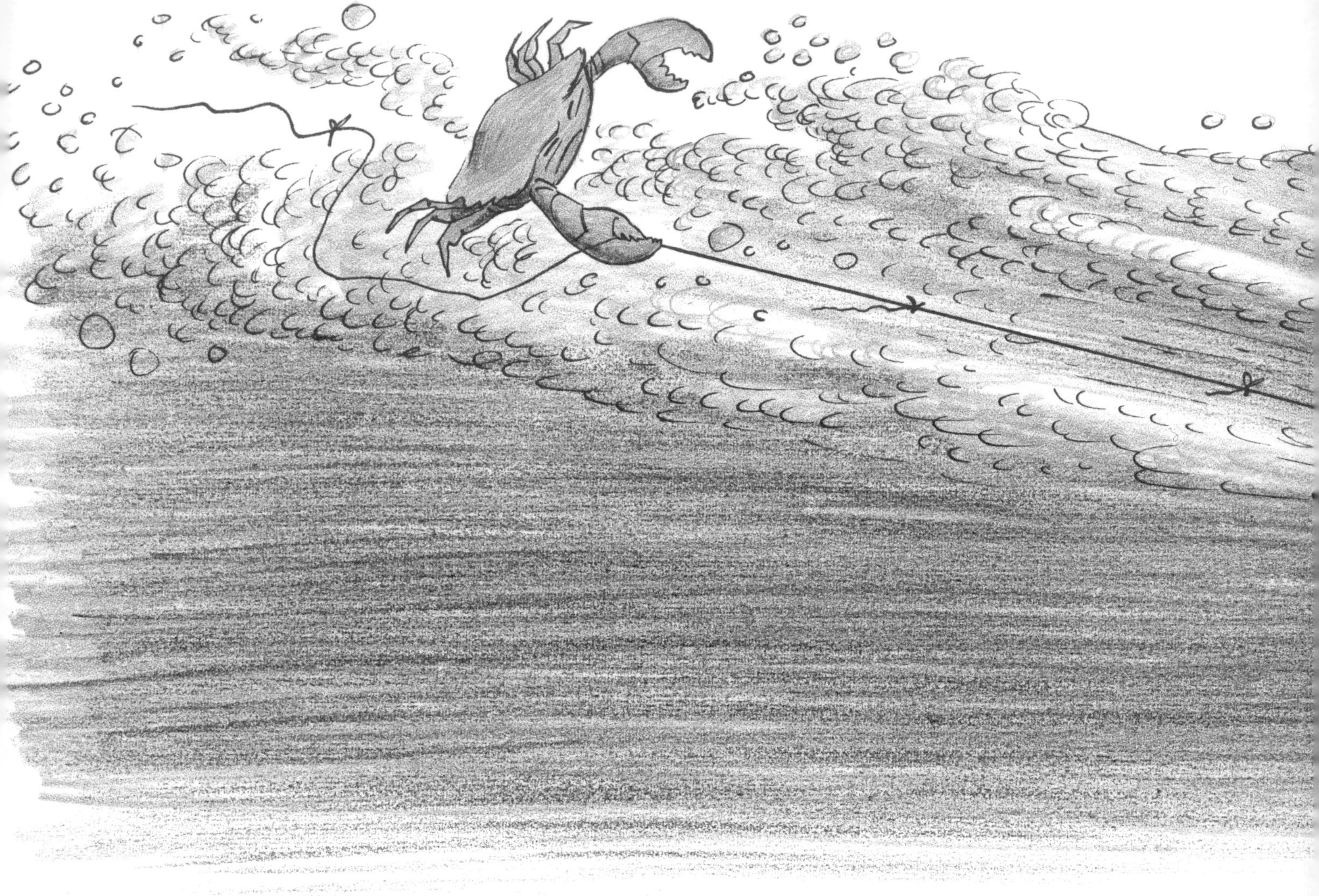

When he found he'd been hooked he took off like a streak,
And the line which was really too flimsy and weak
Suddenly snapped from the force of the shock
Somewhere behind Kermit back near the dock.
He was on his own now, with no one to help,
And off he went flying through tangles of kelp

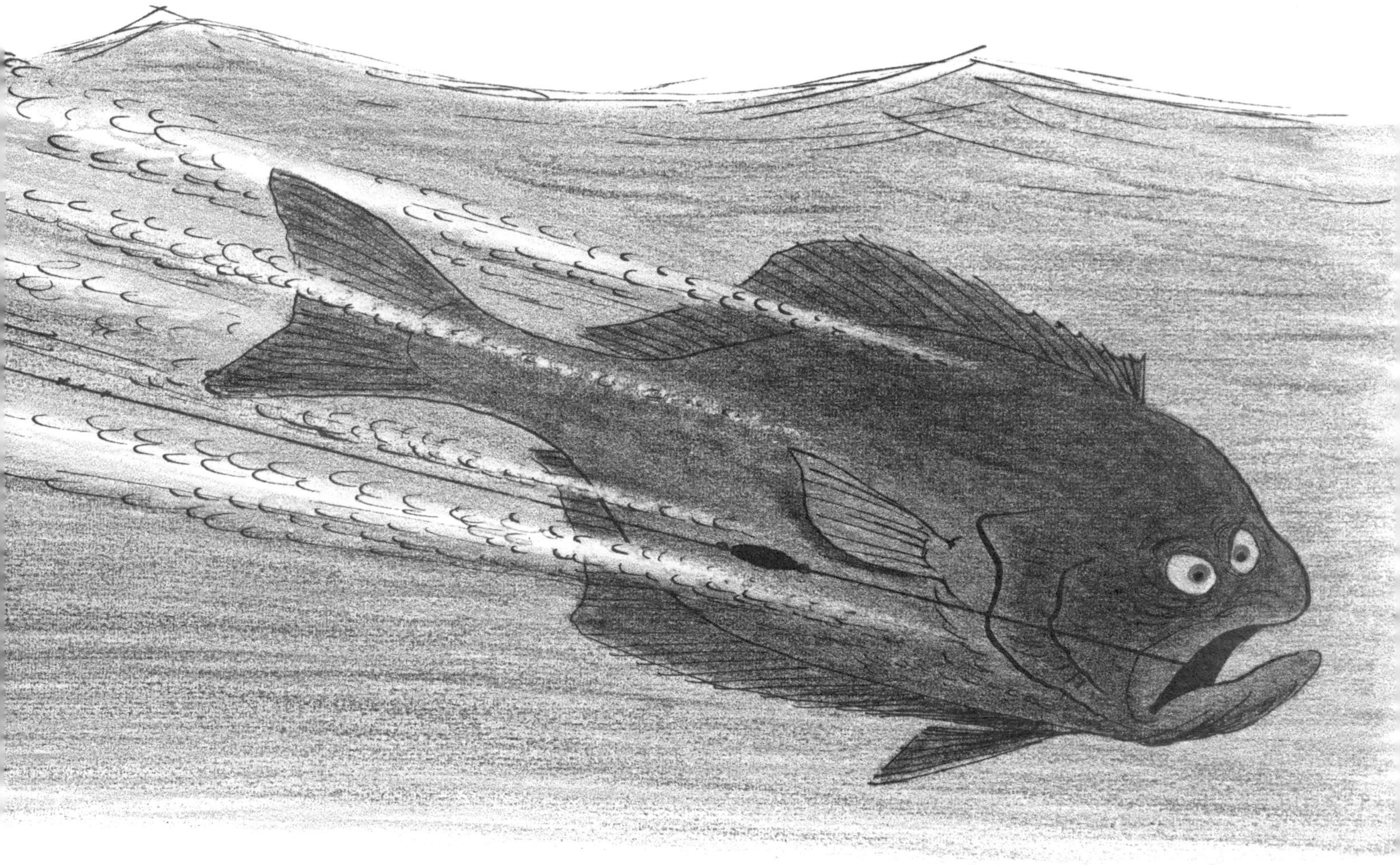

Up over the waves he went floppity flip
Straight out of the bay on a wild foamy trip.
Then somewhere far out in the broad rolling sea
The furious fish finally fought his way free.

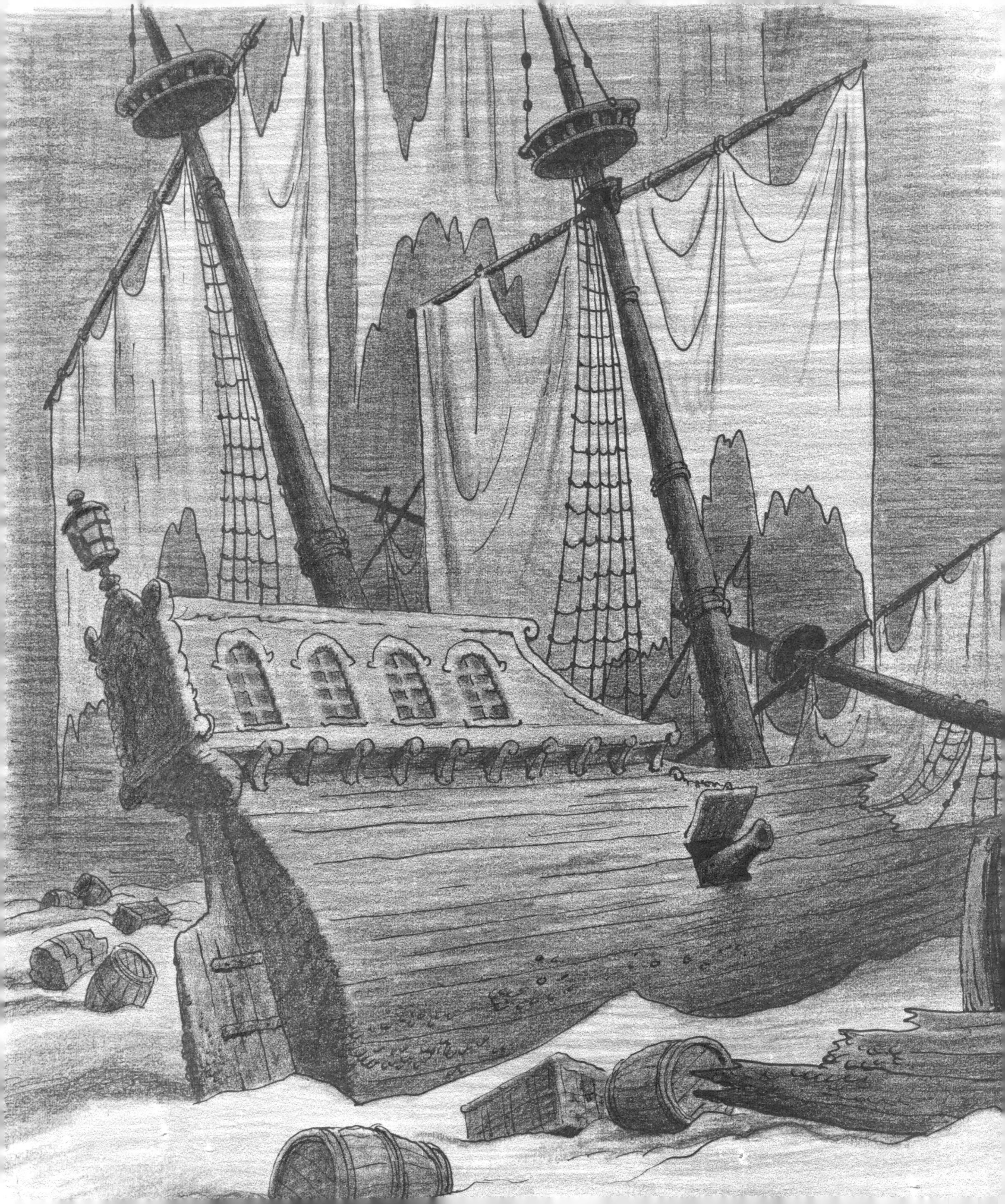

Way out in deep water the crab couldn't crawl,
About all he could do was to let himself fall
And Kermit went tumbling down in slow motion
Into the dark gloomy depths of the ocean.
To the soft sandy floor where he lit with a "plunk"
Near the place where an old pirate ship had been sunk.
The huge hull had been smashed, all the sails ripped and tattered,
And in every direction the cargo was scattered.

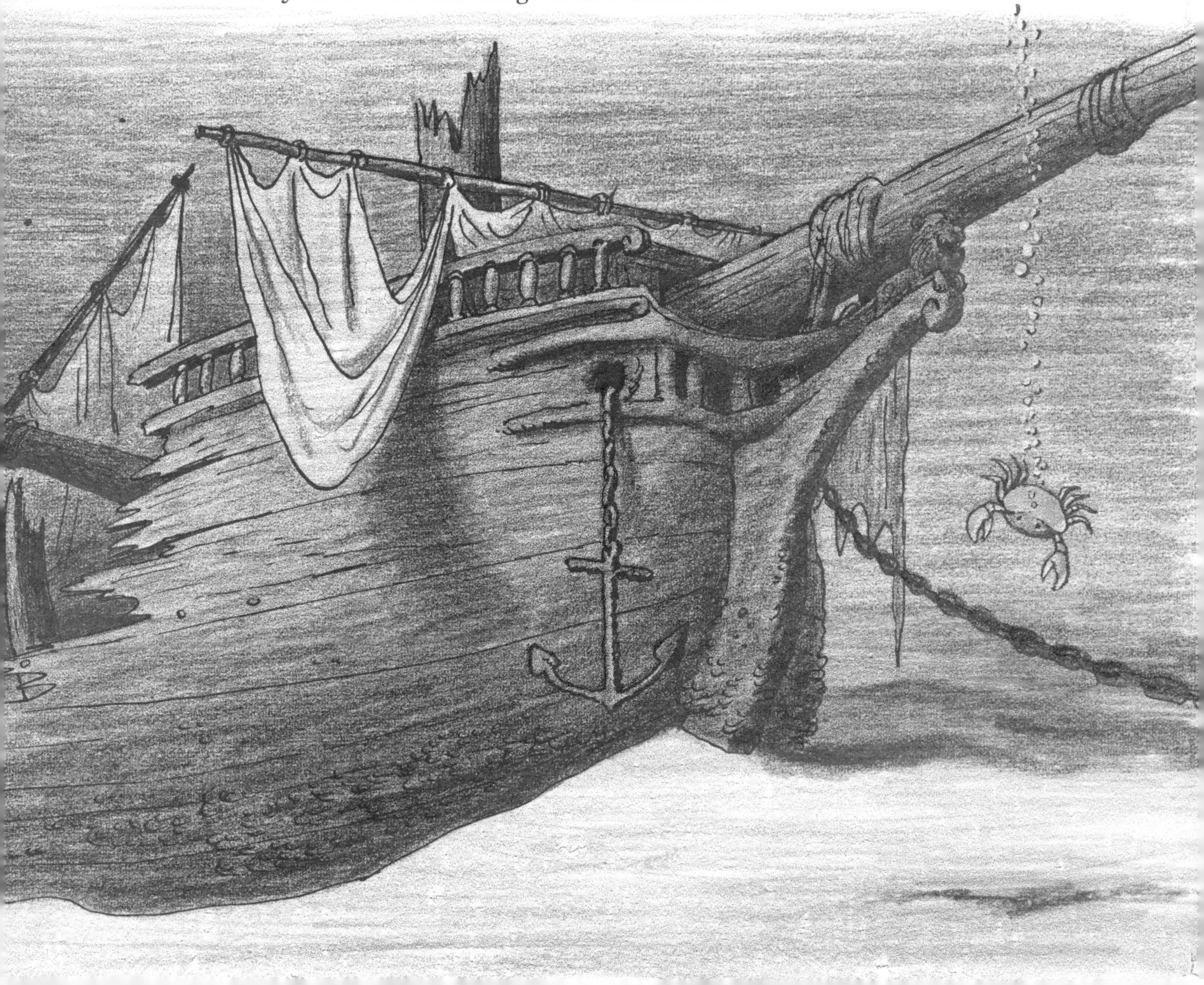

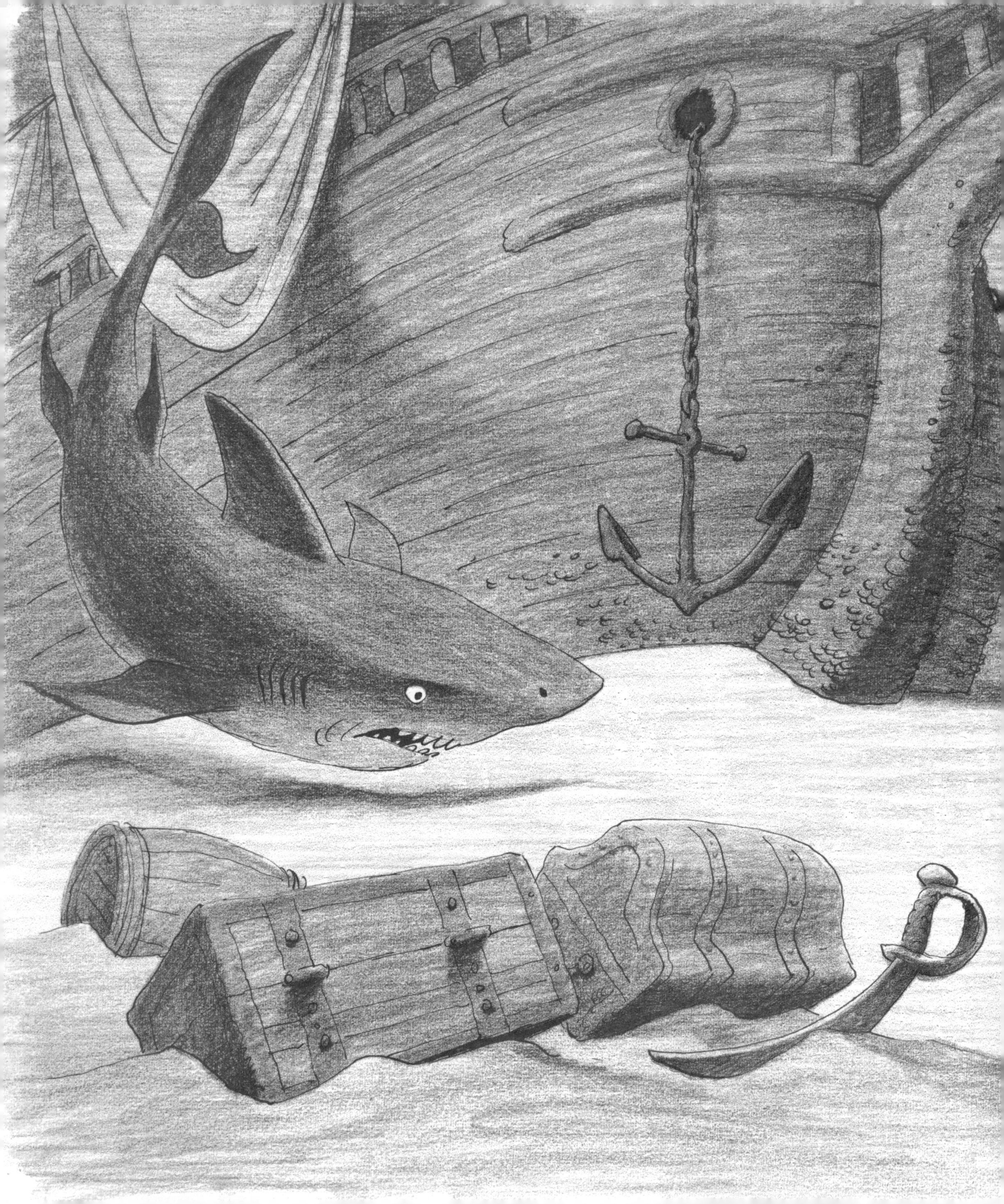

"I imagine," said Kermit, "I'm not safe down here.
"There's much more to this place than the weird atmosphere."
Some creature was watching, the old crab could tell,
By the cold creepy feeling that ran through his shell.
Crouching flat in the sand he peered into the dark
He suddenly saw it—a monstrous blue shark.
As the shark wheeled around for a head-on attack,
Kermit spied an old chest that was open a crack.
He got there a second before the shark did
And in a wild scramble squeezed under the lid.

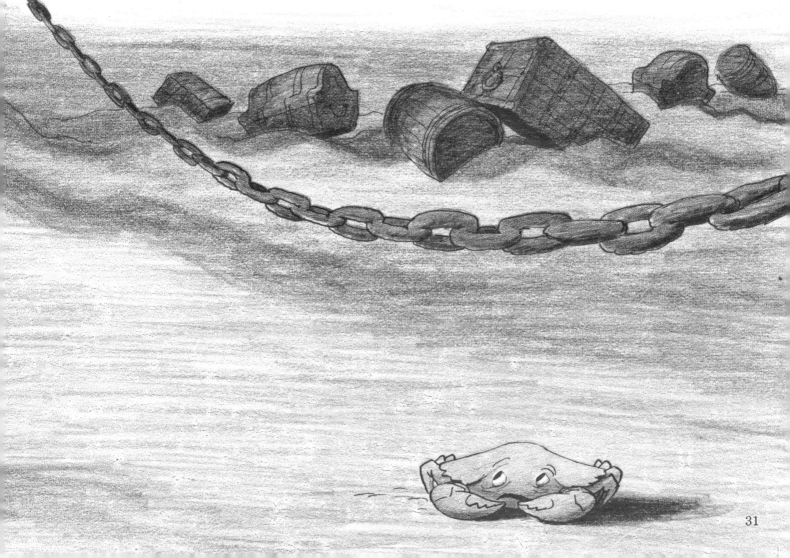

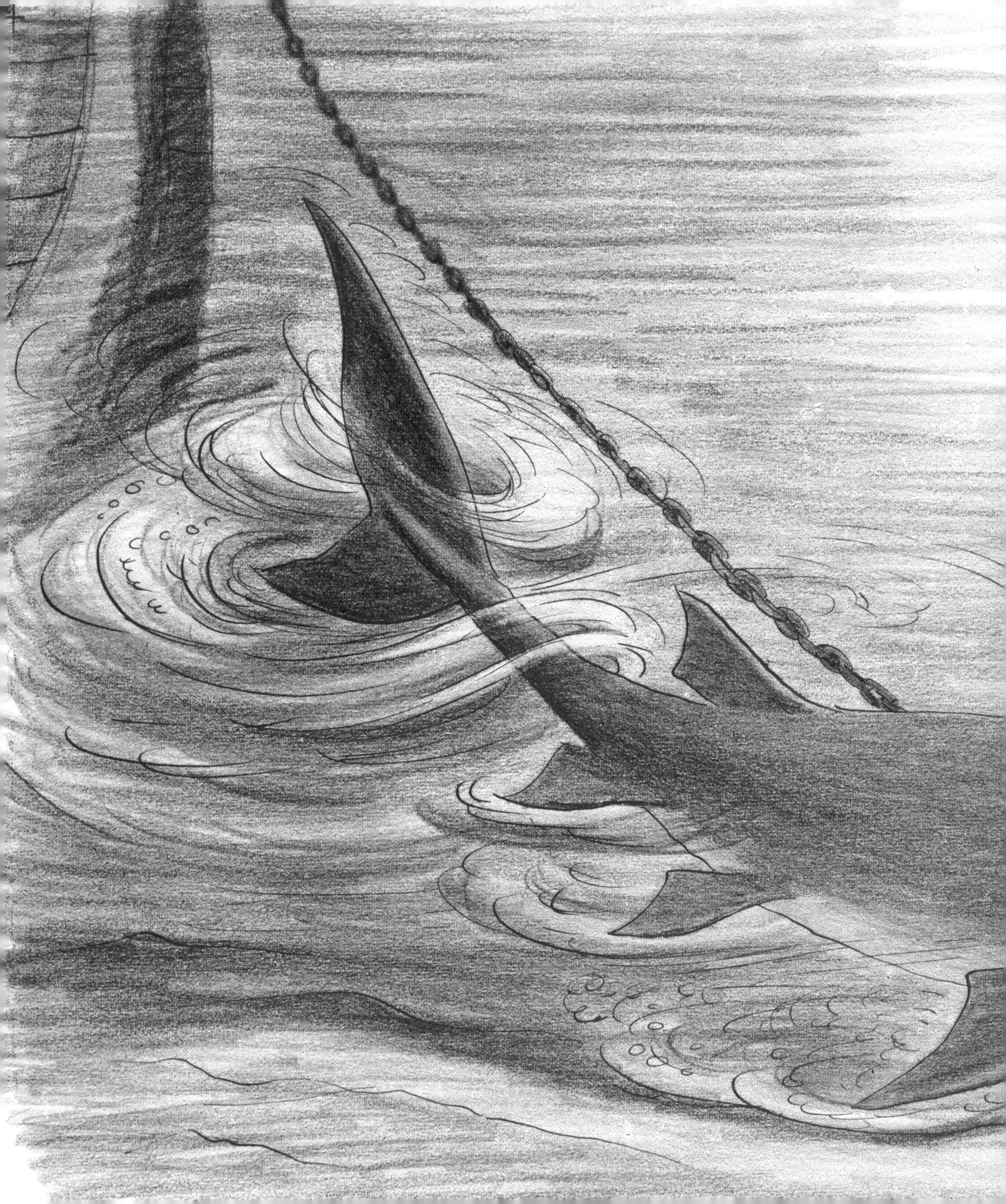

Pushing hard with his snout the big fish tried his best
To force up the lid of the heavy old chest.
He lunged with a fury and all the brute strength
Of his broad fins and tail and his twenty-foot length,
But the lid's double hinges were solid with rust
And a century's thickness of barnacle crust;
So the crab stayed within while the shark stayed without.
All he got for his pains was a badly bruised snout
And he finally turned tail, then away he went tearing
In search of a school of sardines or some herring.

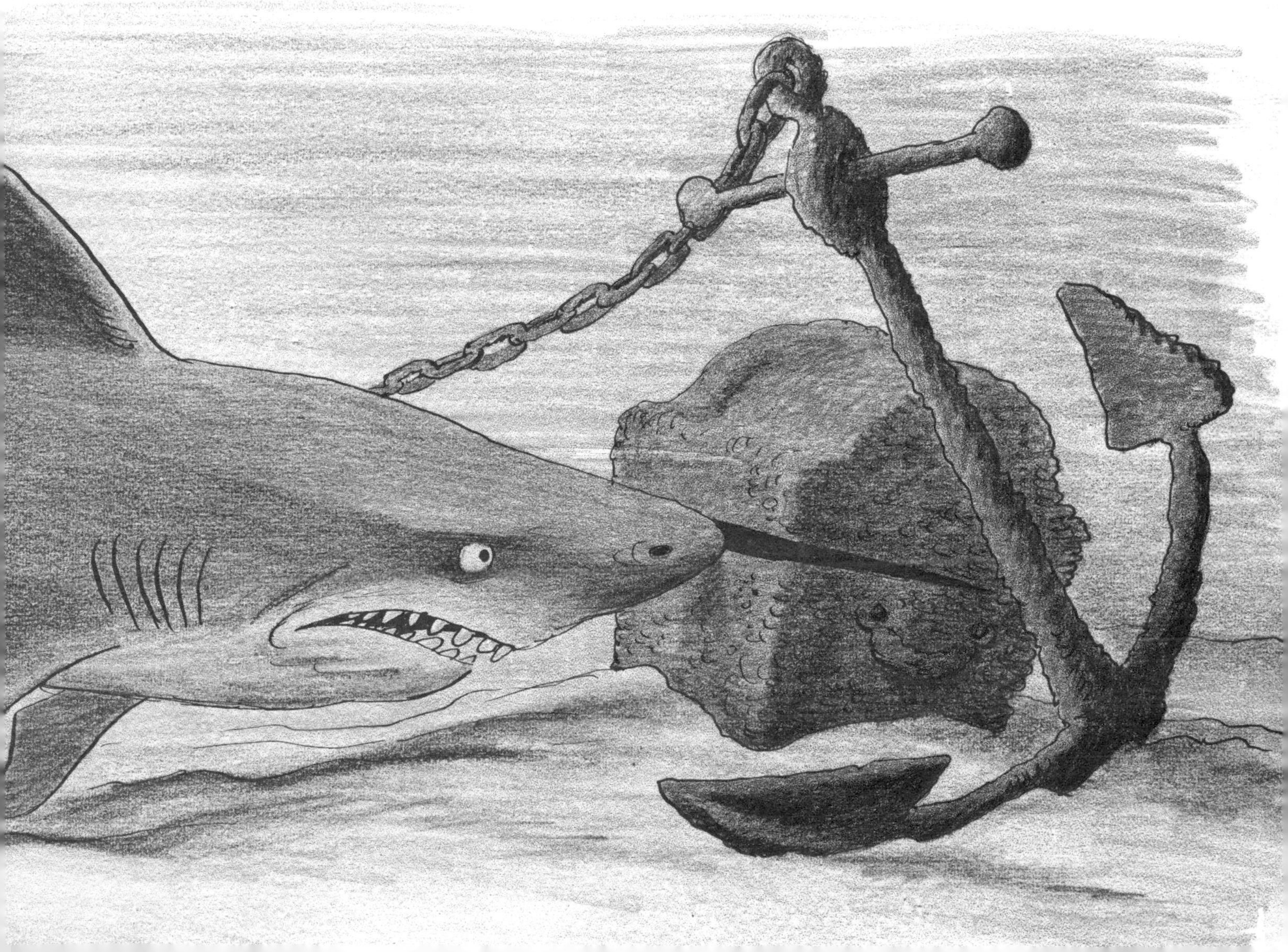

Not until he was sure the big shark was long gone
Did Kermit look down to see what he sat on.
The old chest was filled pretty near to the top
With a heap of gold pieces that made his eyes pop.
"How strange," Kermit muttered, "no one's found it before
"It can't be much more than two miles from shore;
"But anyway all this gold treasure's mine now
"If I just haul it back to my castle somehow."
With a coin in each claw he set out for the bay
With his life in great danger each step of the way.

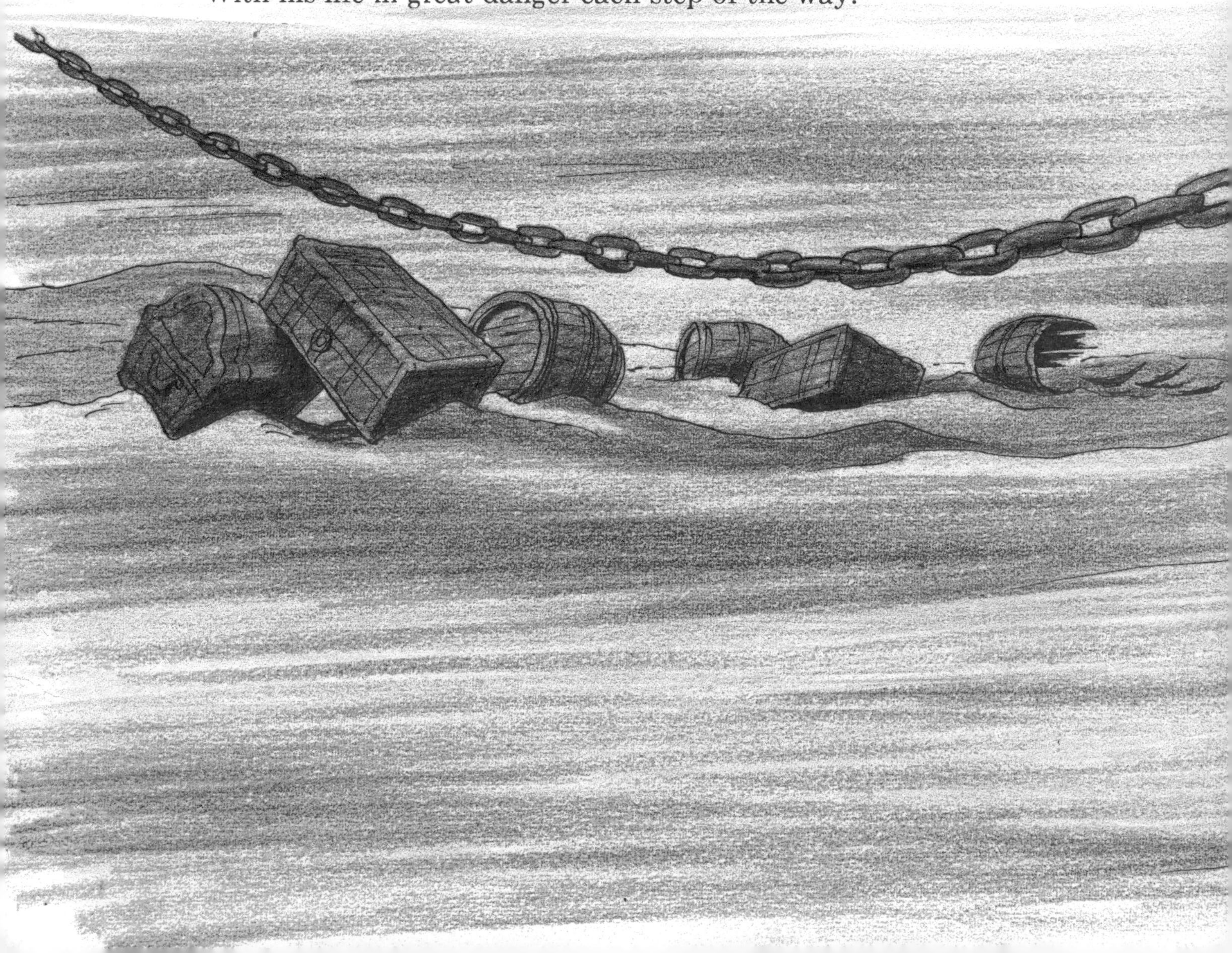

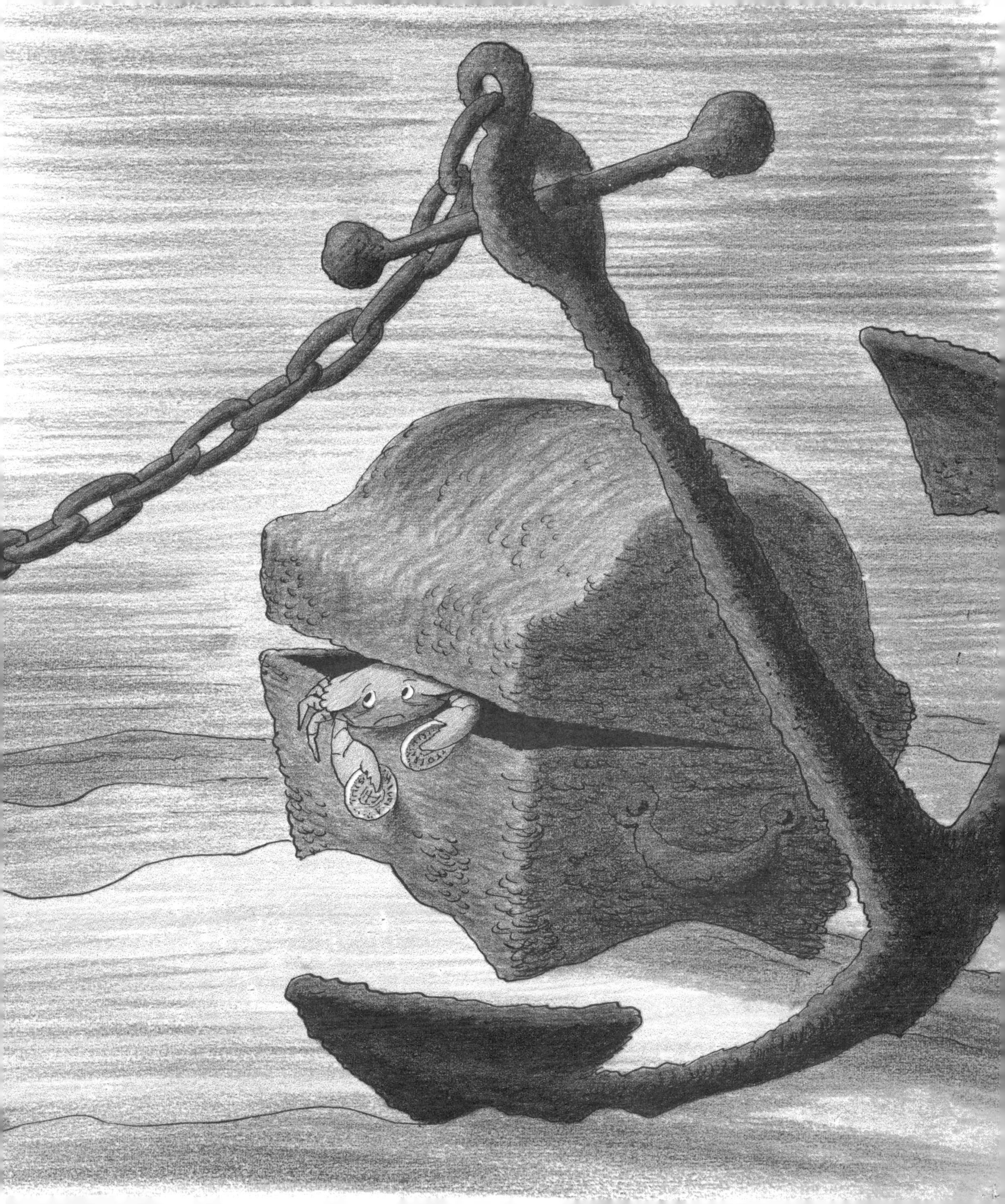

Not only the shark, other big fish as well
Can easily bite through a crab's crusty shell.
To avoid being caught by these crab-hungry enemies,
He scuttled behind the dense clumps of anemones.
Here the deep shadows were mostly blue green
So a bluish green crab there could scarcely be seen.
Every day for three months Kermit made the round trip
Returning each time with two coins in his grip.
To make room for the treasure he emptied his cave
Of the rubble he'd gone to such trouble to save.

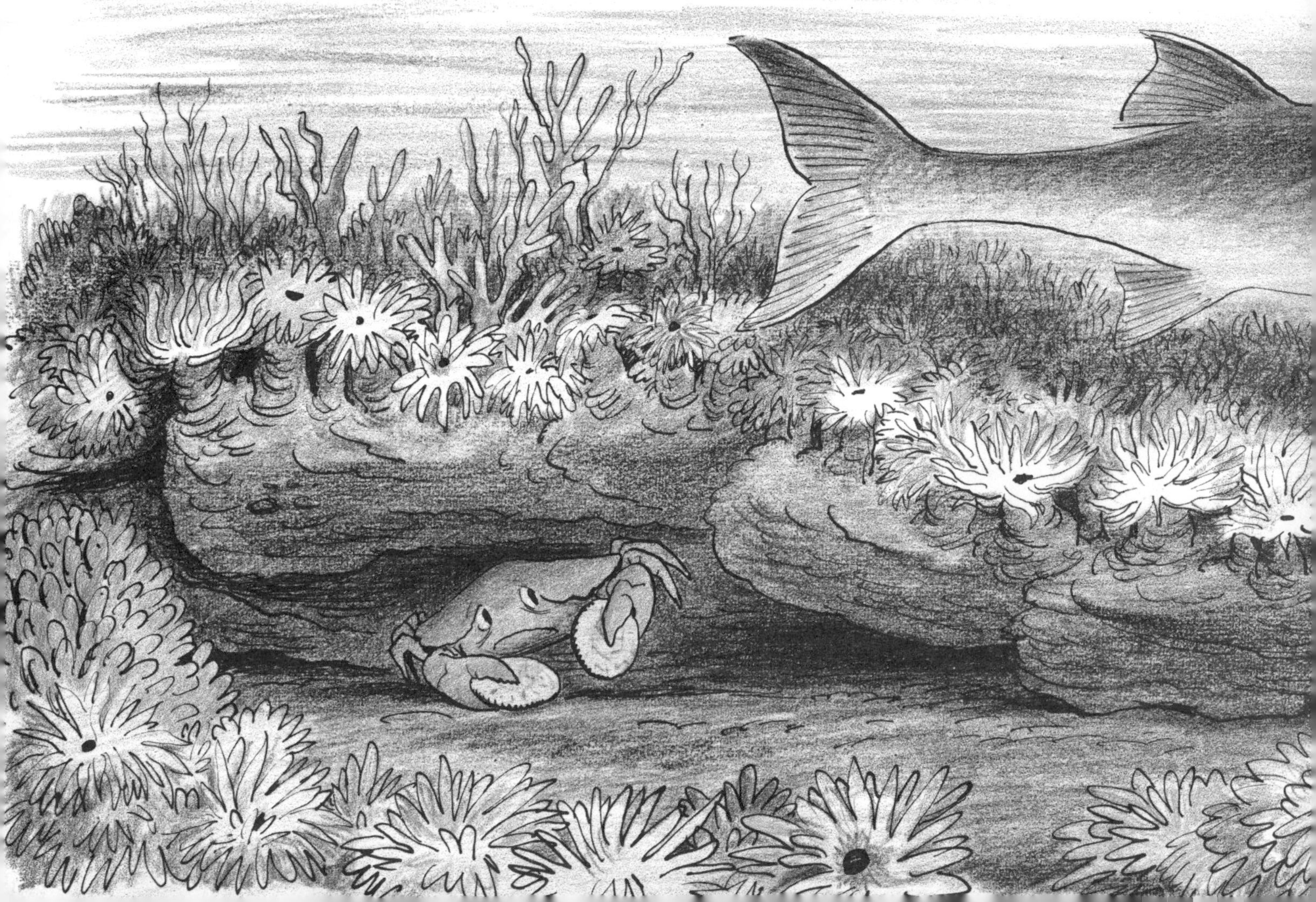

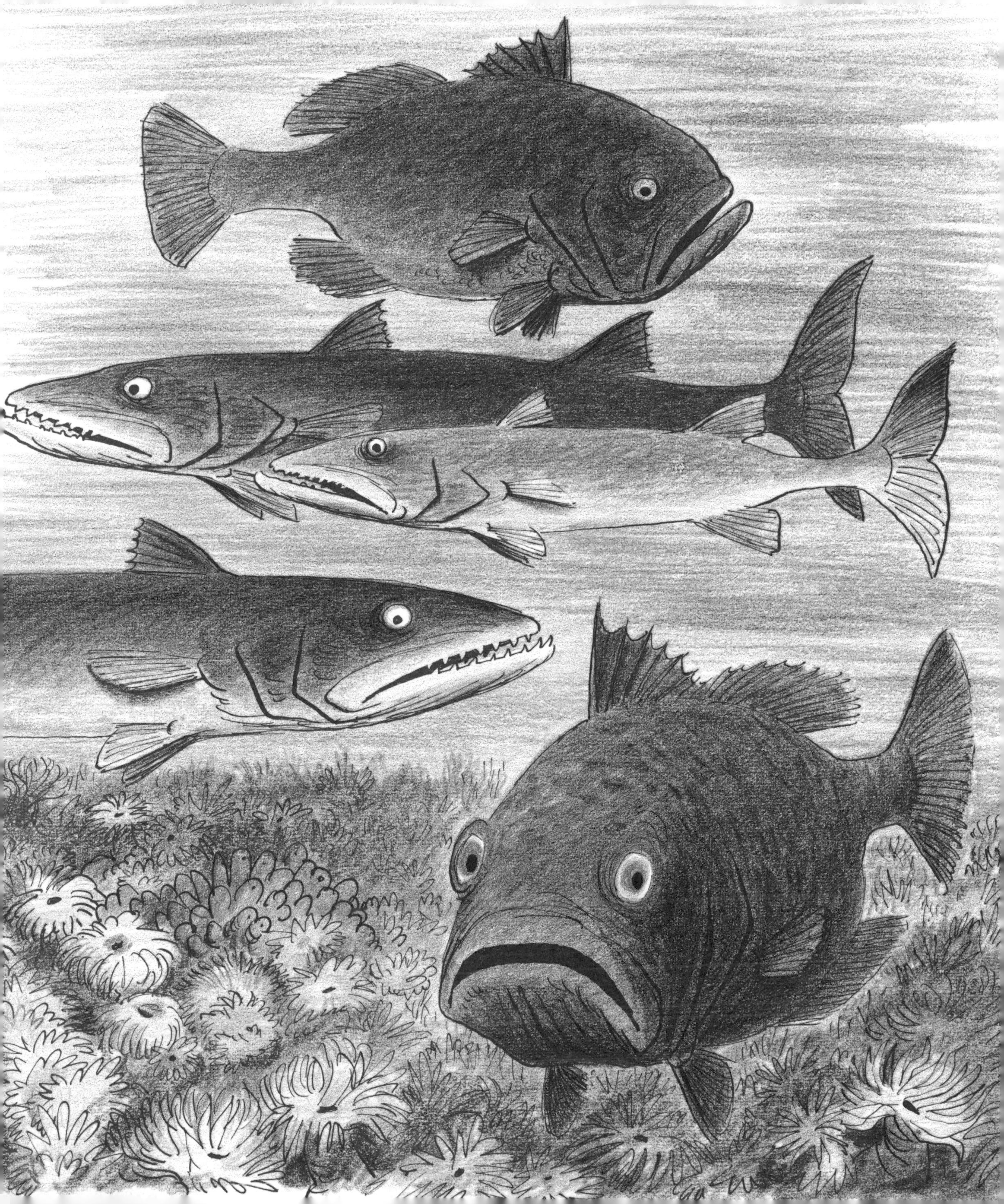

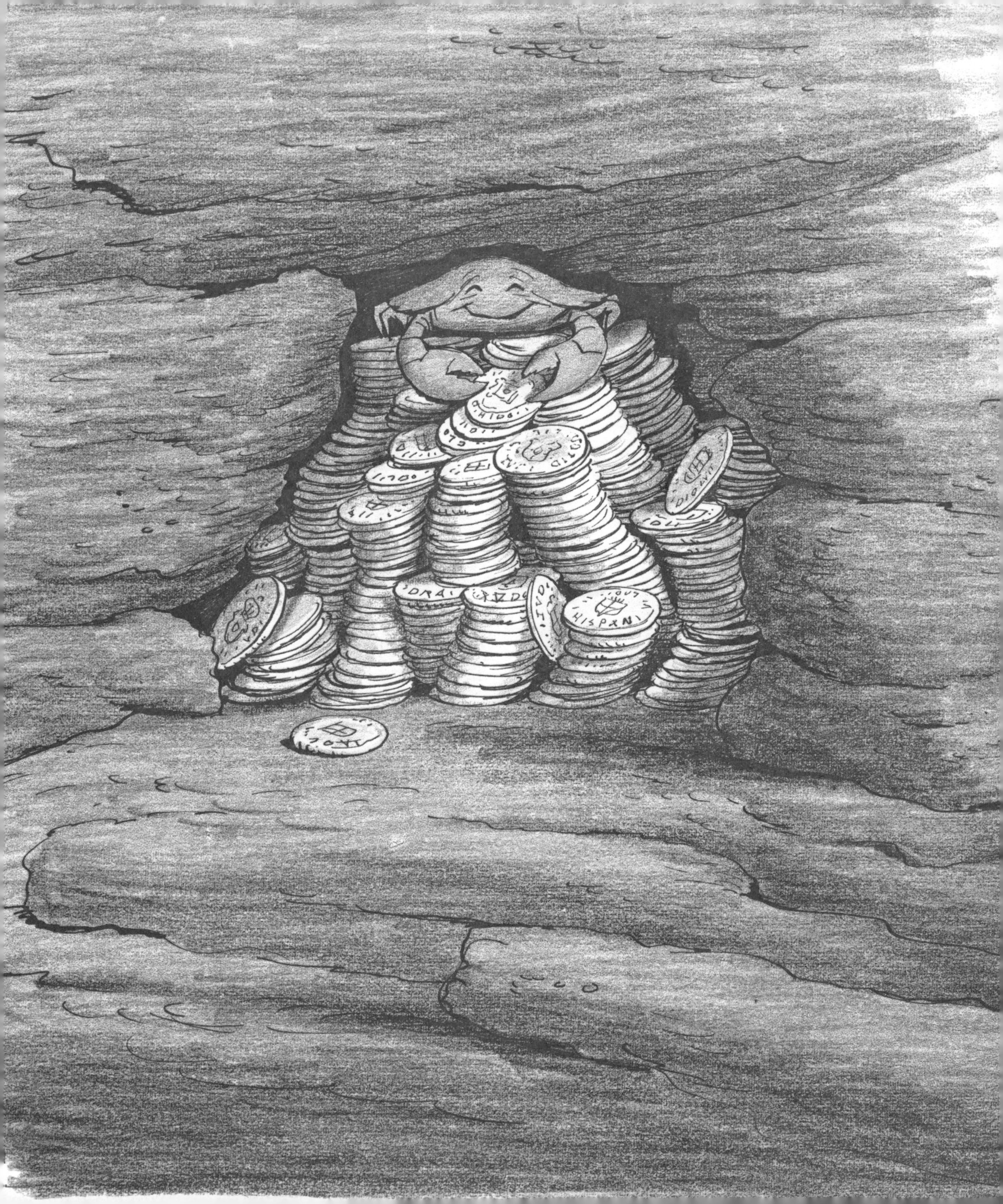

After stacking the gold into one gleaming pile,
His crusty face cracked in a satisfied smile.
He was thinking of all the great pleasure and fun
Such a treasure would bring to a certain someone.
Then he crawled from his cave for a view of the bay
In hopes that he'd find his young friend there that day.

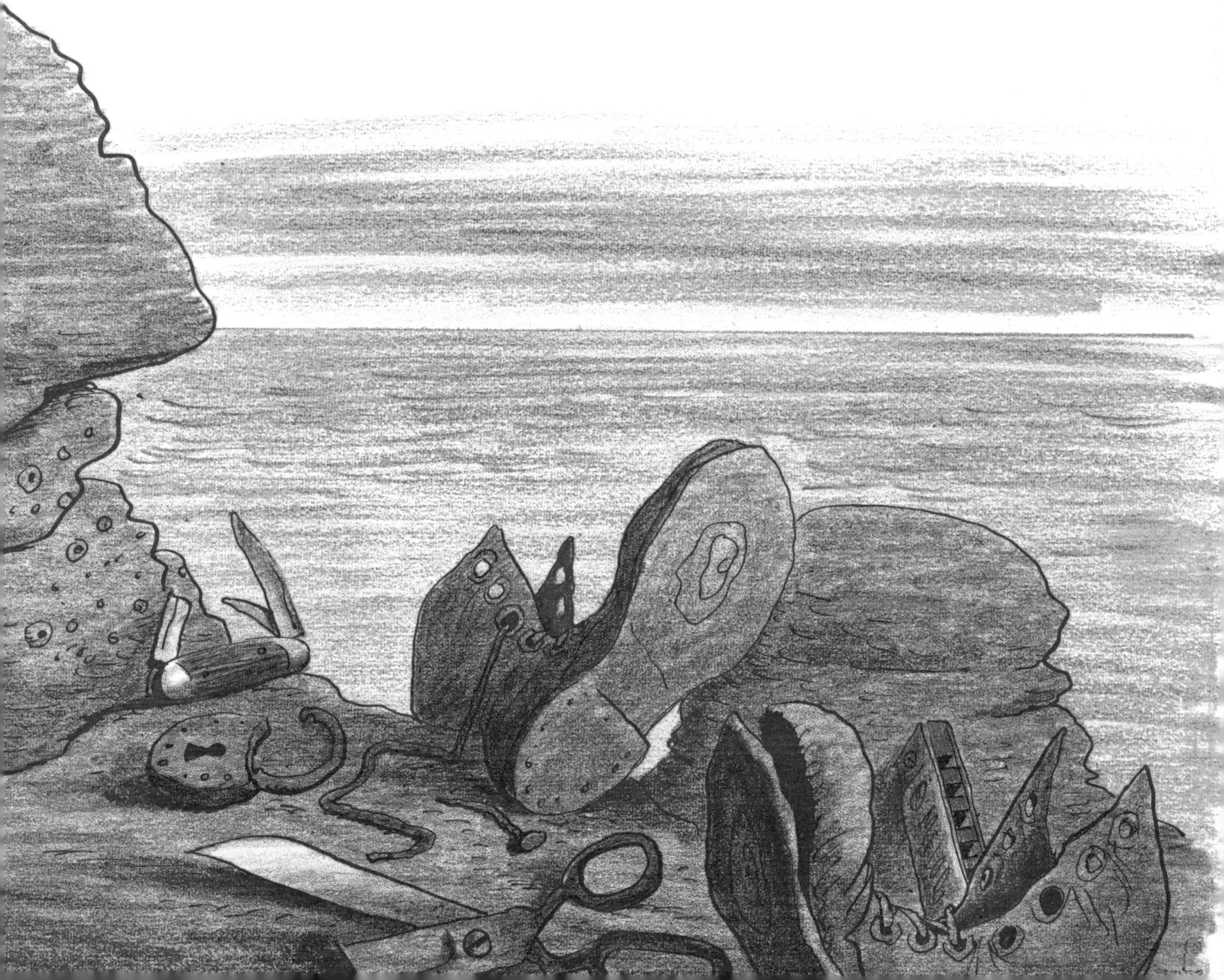

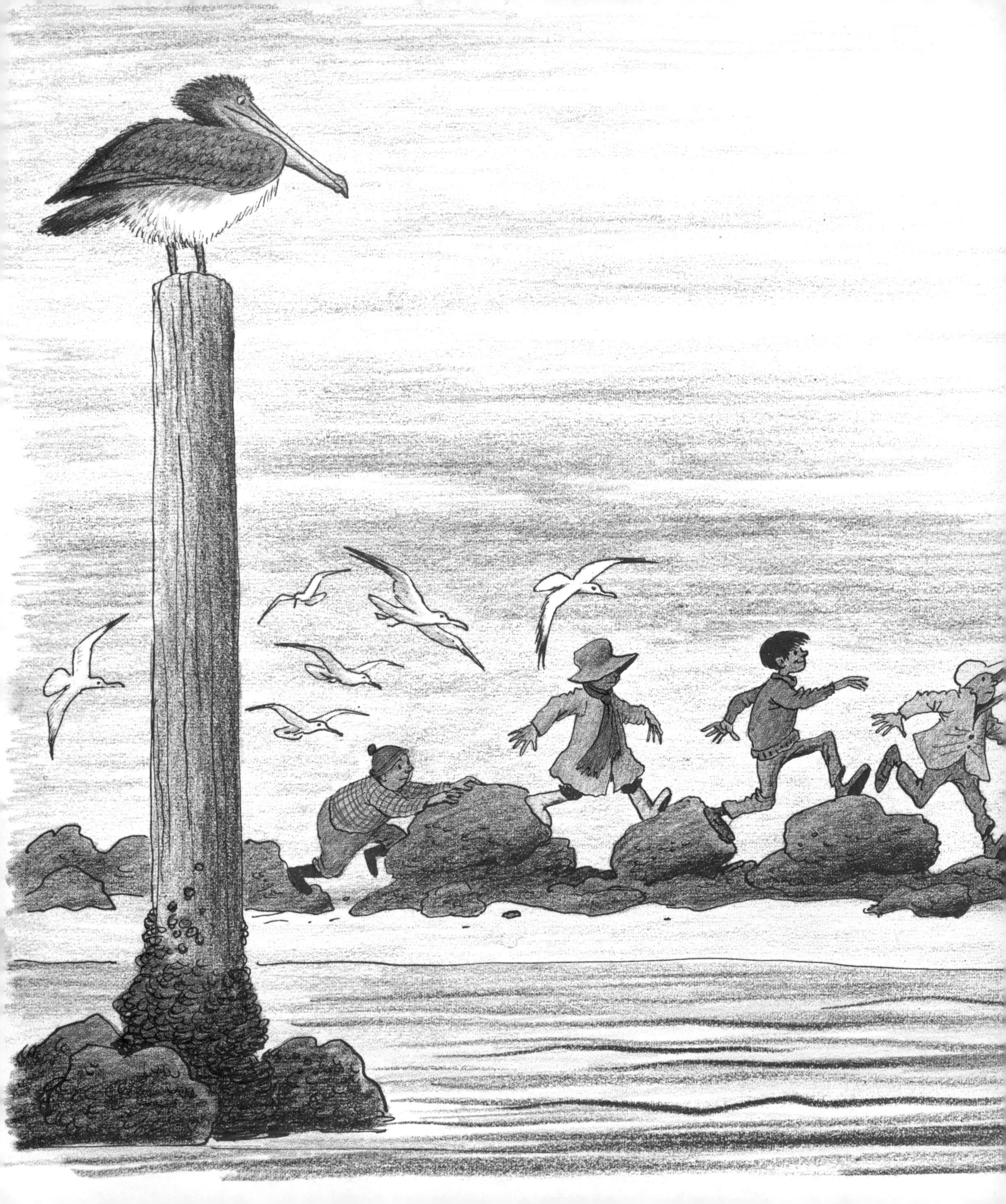

Since the dock was deserted, he looked toward the shore
Where he spied some small boys, half a dozen or more—
Tall ones and scrawny ones, one who was fat,
But not one of them wore a striped shirt or straw hat.
But his young friend might wear something else altogether
Since the winter had come with its cold foggy weather.
"But anyway," Kermit thought, "what could I do?
"Just walk up and say, 'Here's a present for you'?"
Then he heaved such a deep and most sorrowful sigh
He attracted a pelican roosting nearby.

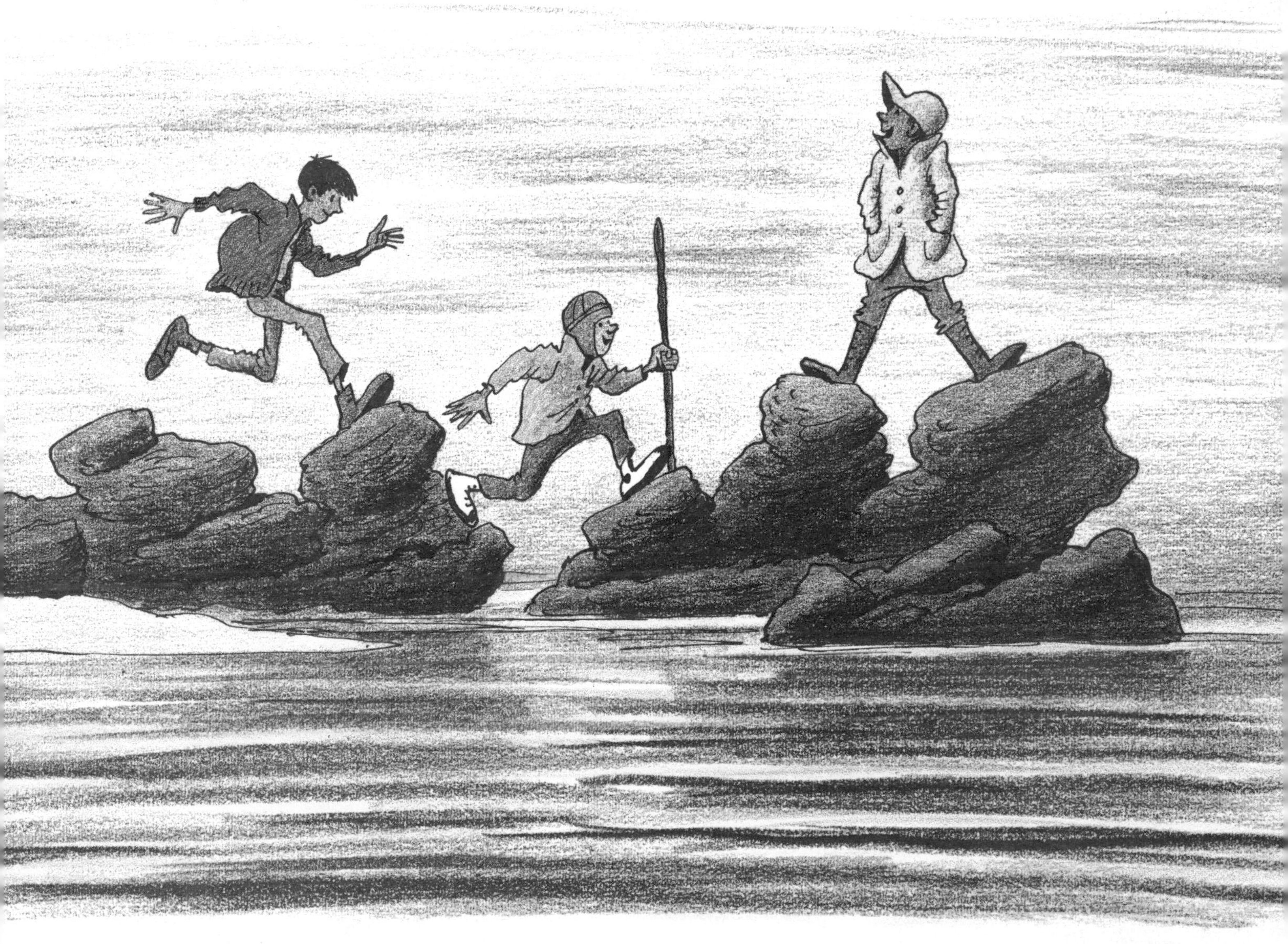

"Now cheer up, old fellow," the big bird began
Smiling as only a pelican can.
"If you've got a problem, please let me suggest
You tell it to me—get the thing off your chest."
No one could resist such a friendly big smile;
So the crab told his tale to him after a while,
Showed all the gold when he came to the end,
Then tried to describe his heroic young friend.
"That boy," said the bird, "is familiar to me.
"Some people watch birds; I watch people, you see.
"The lad has two sisters and also one brother
"And then, I'm quite certain, a father and mother.
"They live in a very small three-room red shack
"In the south part of town beside the train track.
"I could carry the treasure there inside my beak
"But I'd swallow it all, for my beak has a leak;
"So if you would like I'll just give you a lift,
"Besides you're the one to deliver the gift."

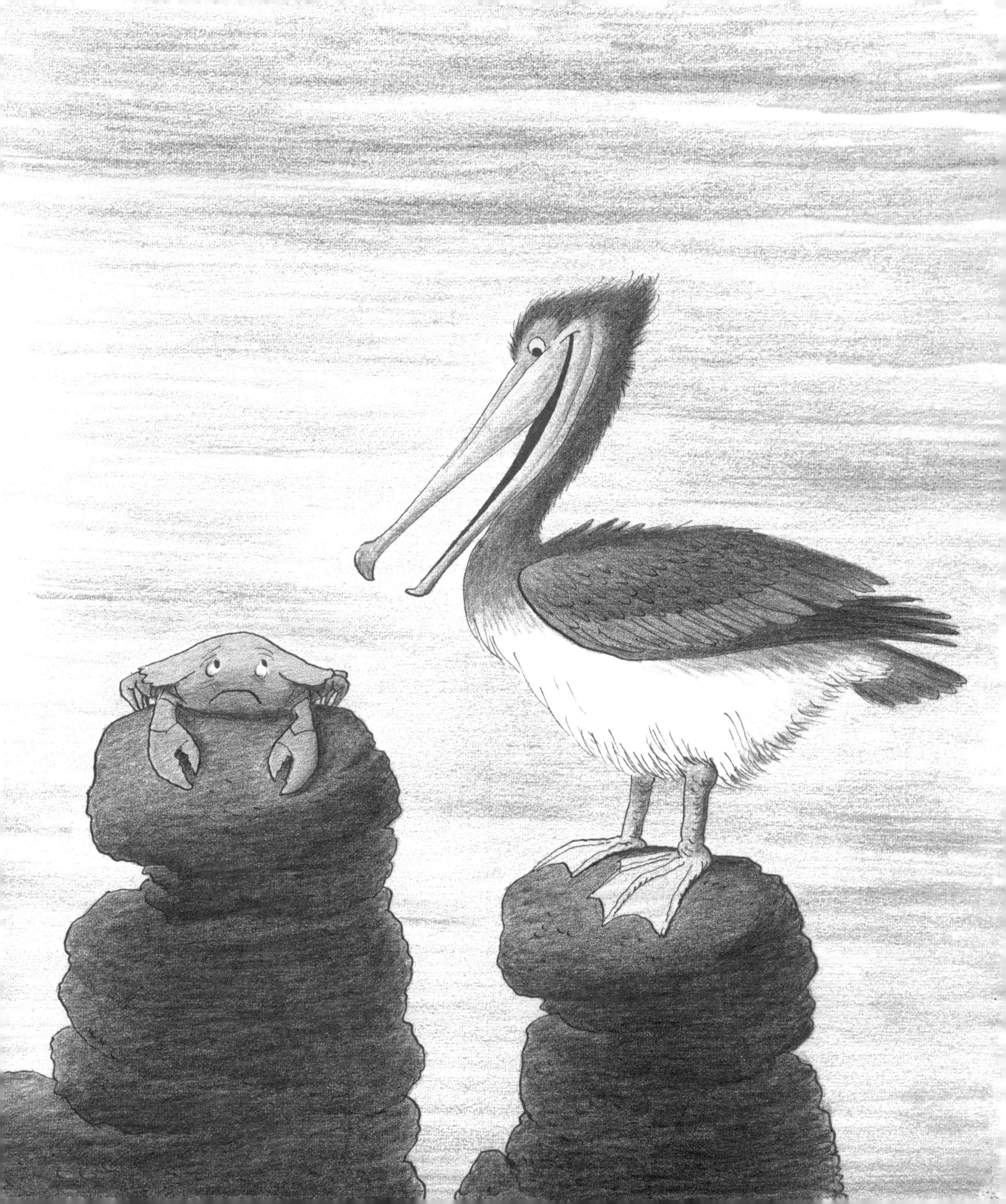

And so with two gold pieces tight in his grip
Kermit took off on his first flying trip
Across the broad bay in one breath-taking swoop
Away through the dense fog as thick as pea soup.
By the time Kermit got up the nerve to look down,
The big bird was soaring out over the town.
Below was a small cottage painted barn red
Beside the train track as the pelican said.
That poor people lived there was easy to see
For it was the one house without a TV.

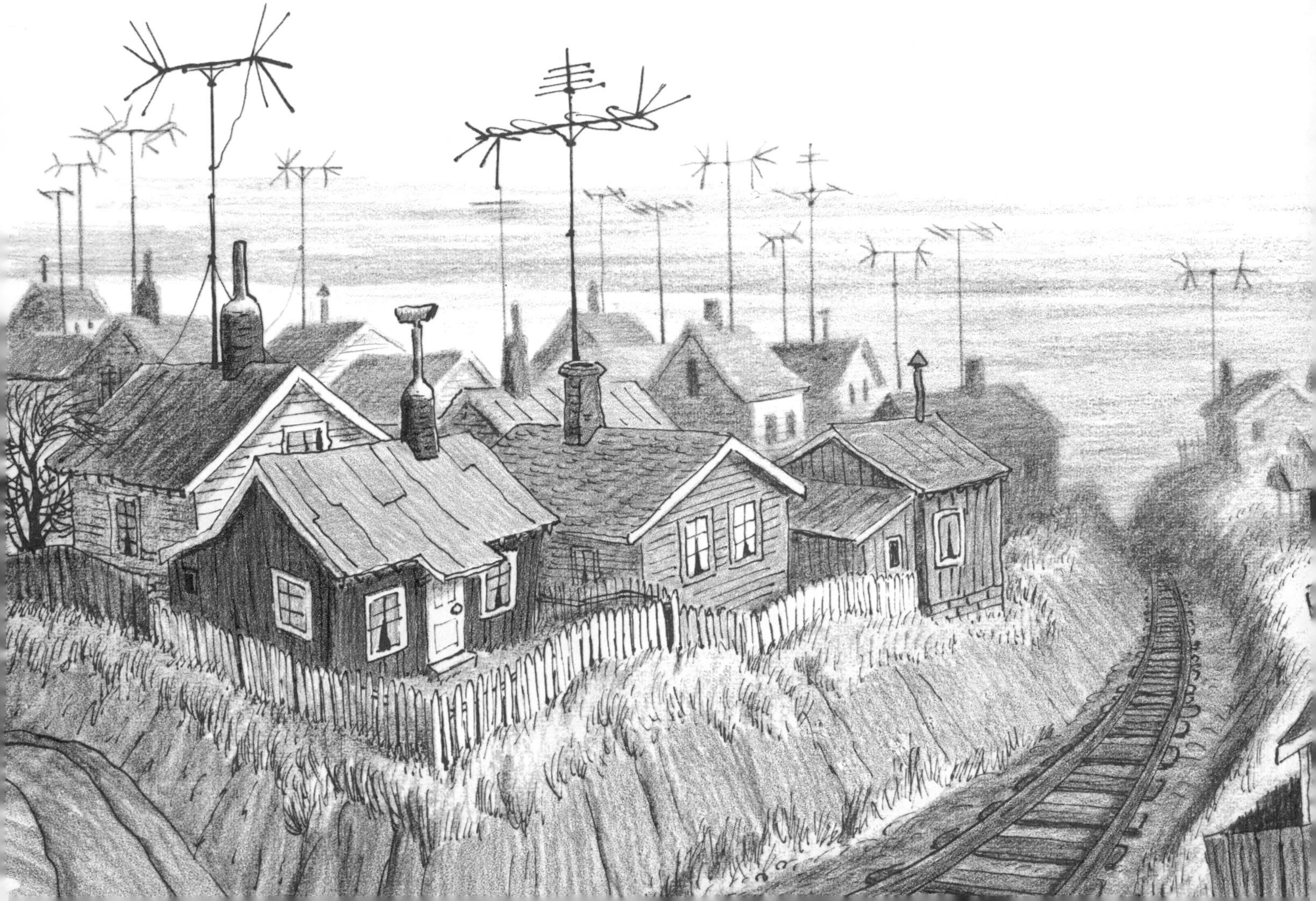

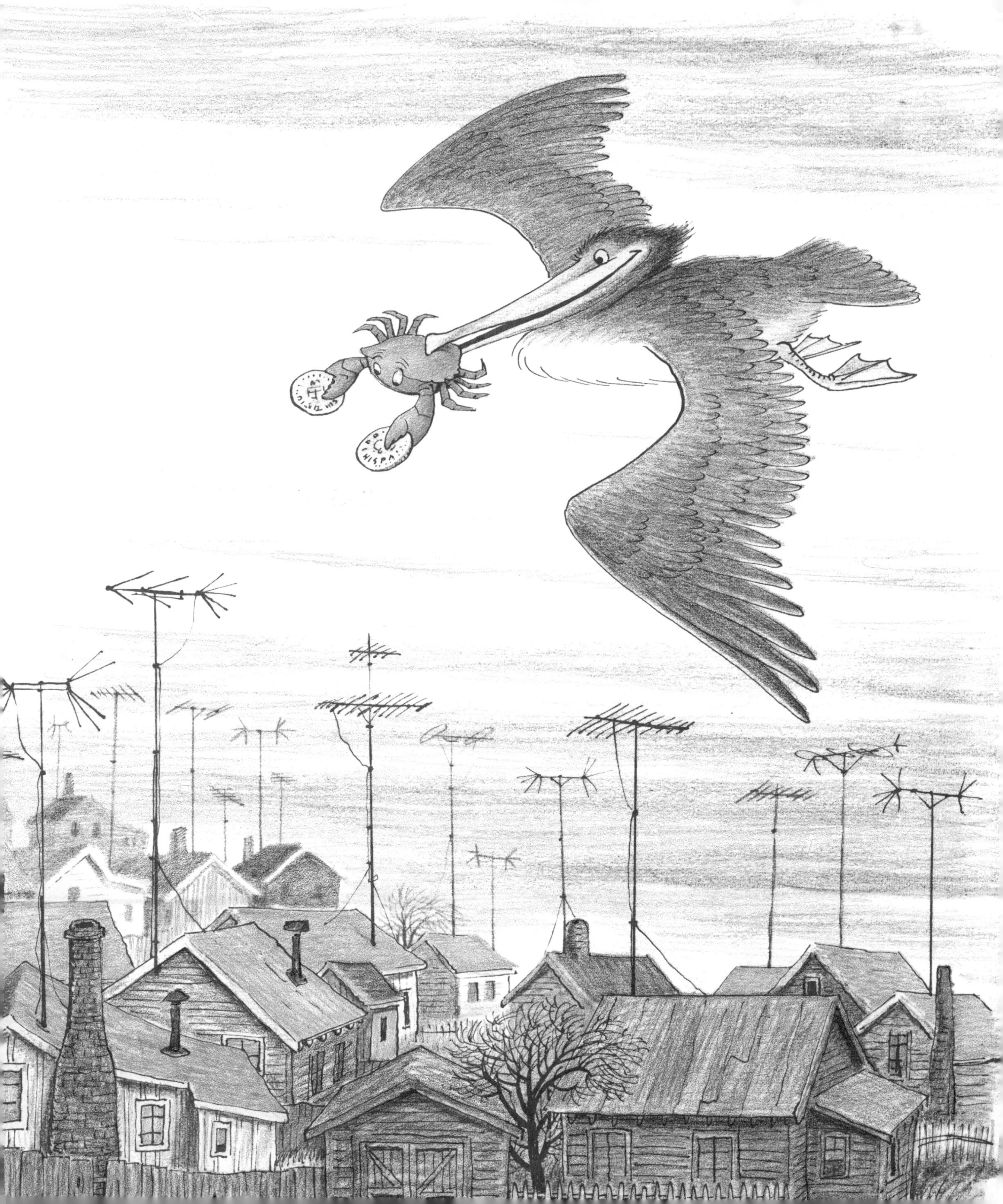

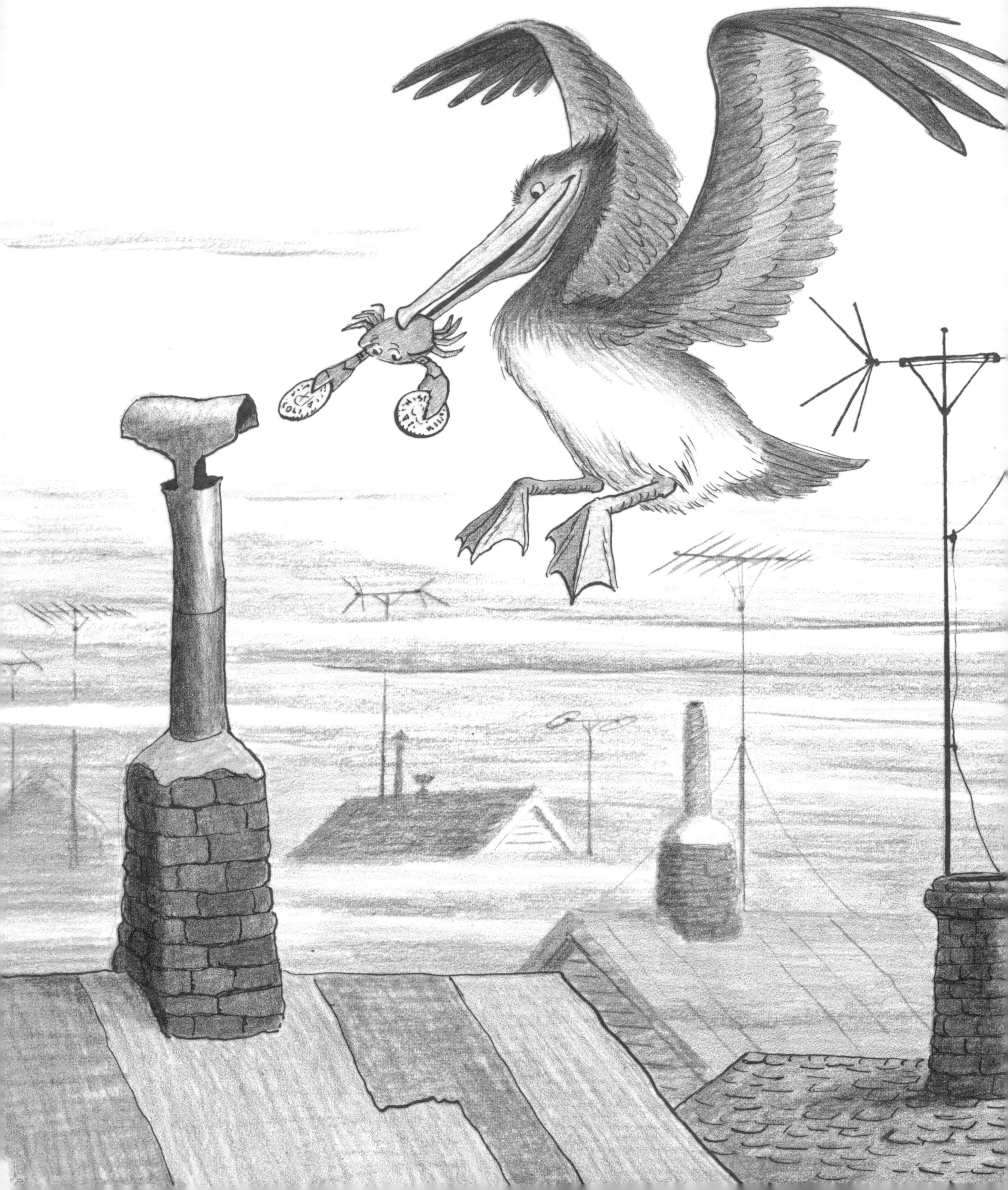

As the pelican came to a fluttering stop
Alongside the chimney, he let the coins drop.
They fell to the bottom, the two friends could tell,
For the pot-bellied stove went "ker bong!" like a bell.
Then inside the house great excitement broke out,
"Why it's gold, it's real gold," they heard somebody shout.

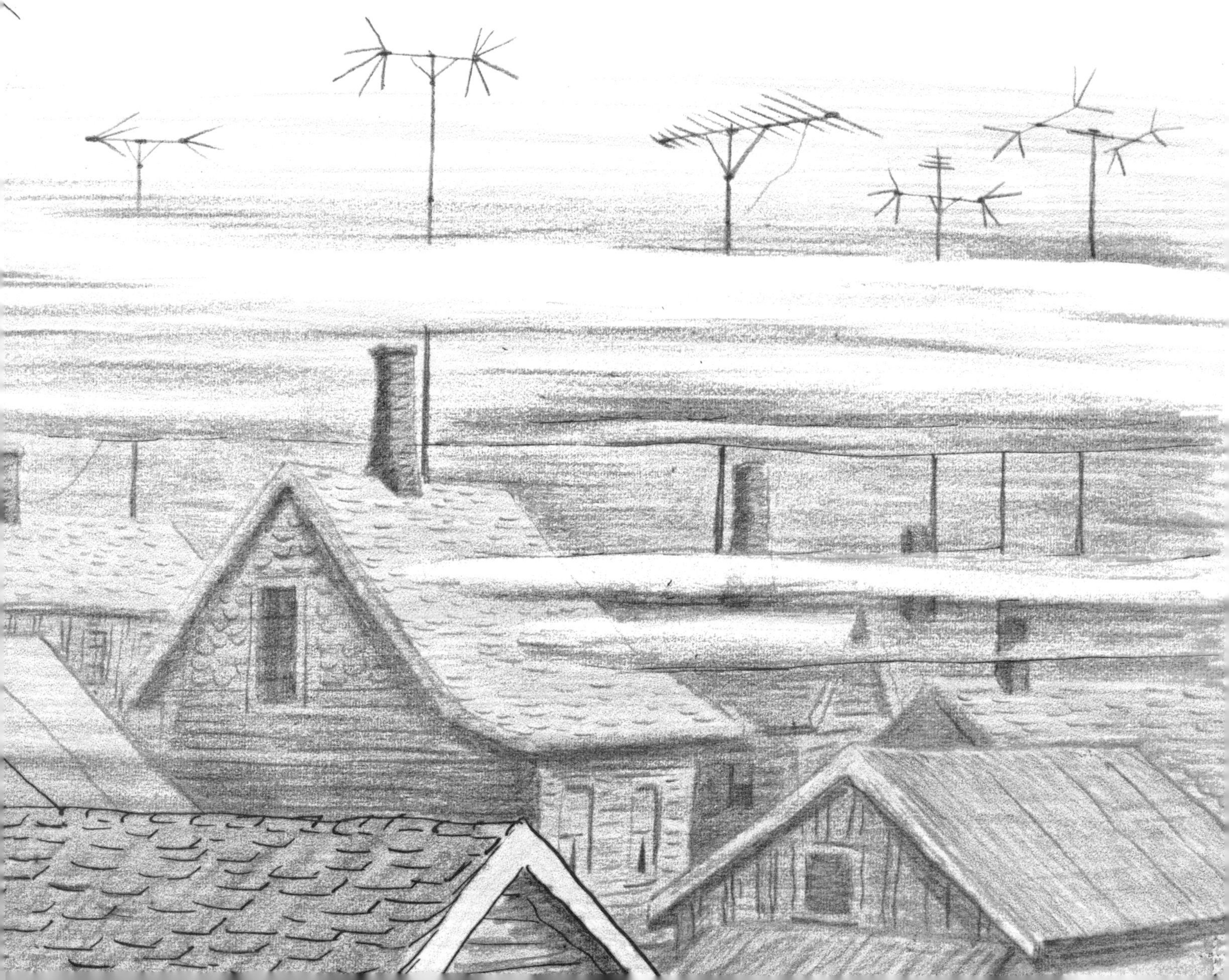

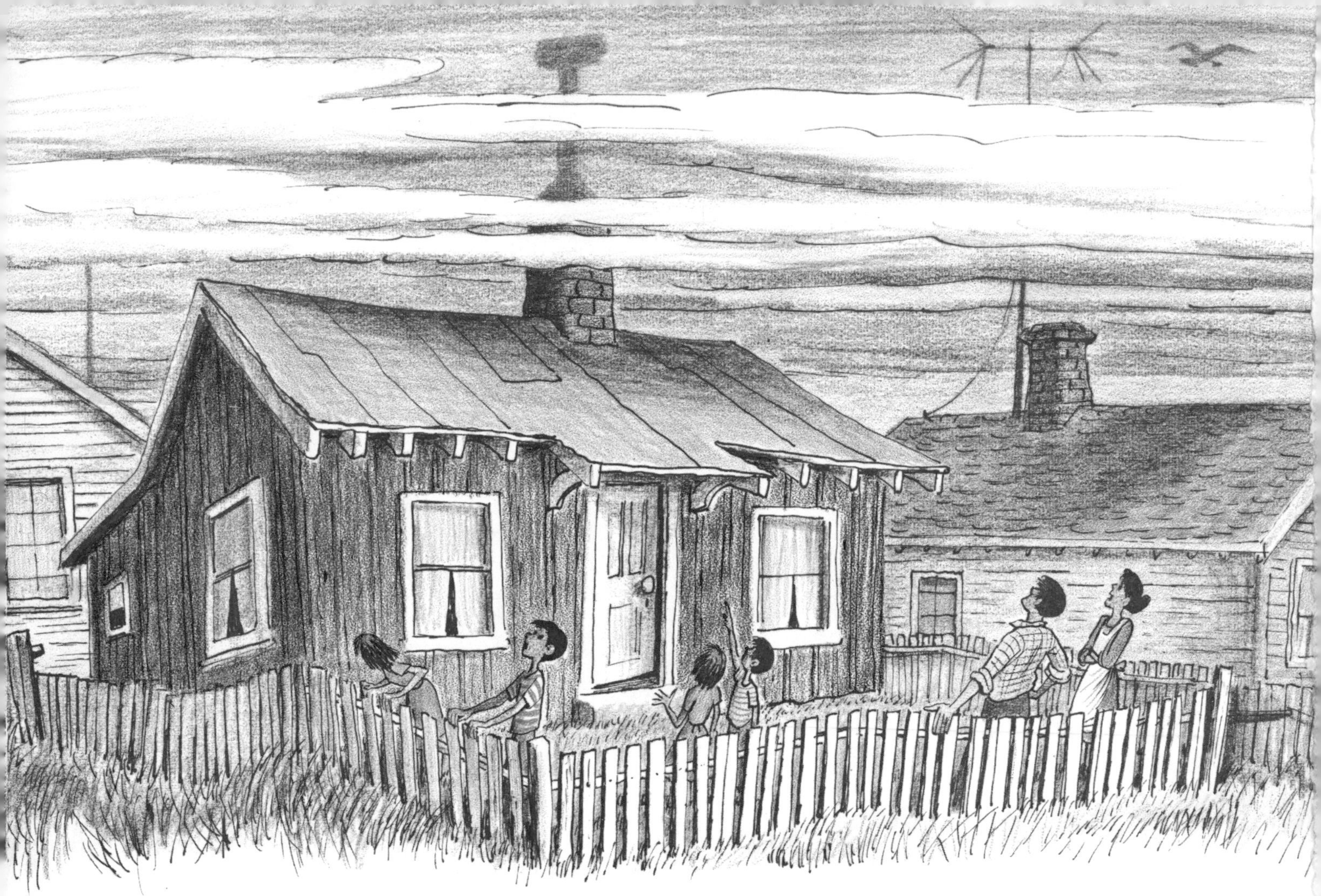

The family ran out to find what it could be
But discovered the fog had rolled in from the sea.
A ghostly white curtain closed in everywhere
So they never caught sight of whoever was there.
The high-flying crab in the pelican's beak
Brought the family a fortune inside of a week.
Soon they had a TV set and all sorts of toys,
Such as dolls for the daughters and bikes for the boys.
All the rest of the gold which was quite an amount
They set safely aside in a savings account,
For the wise father said, "It is not every day
"That a fortune is dropped down our chimney that way."